SPONTANEOUS COMBUSTION
VOLUME 1

Second Edition, July 2012

Copyright © 2012 by Sic Semper Serpent

Published by
Sic Semper Serpent
P.O. Box 8847
Minneapolis, MN 55408-8847

For the People | By the People
www.sicsemperserpent.com

Printed in the United States of America

The Publisher wishes to thank:

Michael Strand
Julia Crouse
Ben Ubl
Janet Kolterman
Bennett Smith
Amber Davis
Magers & Quinn

CONTENTS

Contents

PREFACE

Warning: This book made in one day. That's right, the tales within were written during one 24-hour period. Nothing considered sacred save for the art of Story. If you say Yay! to a folk fiction revival fueled by the writers, the people, and you, then read on.

Spontaneous Combustion (a.k.a. SpoCo) is more like an exercise than it is a book. It gives reason for Twin Cities' area writing talent to flex its muscles. Around 40 brand new pieces of short fiction arrived in our inbox after launching SpoCo at Magers & Quinn in Minneapolis, MN. We narrowed it down to these 11 stories through editorial decision, wicked story slams, and a public poll exactly one week later. On that first night, we gave the writers three prompts, which later amounted to three similarities between all the tales. Can you guess the three common threads running through them all?

So what do you get when you gather a bunch of authors together, give them three prompts, tell them they have one day, and pump them full of caffeine? A thunderous throw-down of literary proportions, that's what. It's fiction of the people, by the people, for the people in the truest sense.

From the harrowing adventure of Frank Sylvester in "Closing the Circle", to the tear jerking realism of "Good to Know", no genre of short story has been overlooked. You may even debunk a conspiracy or two while learning how to properly break and enter. This collection of creative fiction has got it all, but please be aware that we haven't censored a single word or line. So shall the Story reign supreme.

This daring book-in-a-day project seeks to re-imagine the economy of publishing and crush the obstacles many independent authors face today. In a time when language is changing, when doorbells are text messages and laughter is lol, it is important to remember which words resonate deeply with the human spirit. Linguistics can (and will) transform to match society and technology; its rules are transitive and subject to change. But the reason to swap our words will never change: to communicate thoughts and ideas with narrative. Sic Semper Serpent is dedicated to preserving the Story in our contemporary society. We make folklore for the spirit of today. Better yet, we make mythology of the modern age.

If this sounds like the home for you, then join up and speak out! There's no need to go it alone. "Of the people, by the people. Know thy publisher." That's our motto at Sic Semper Serpent. Unlike more conventional publishers, we don't fear the changing state of language. We embrace it; we are bound to it (pun!). Welcome to Spontaneous Combustion. Welcome to Sic Semper Serpent.

Stay Classy,
T. Martin Crouse
Editor-in-Chief
sicsemperserpent.com

CLOSING THE CIRCLE

Nathaniel Hicklin

People used to believe in all sorts of things hundreds of years ago: vampires, werewolves, ghosts, fairies, demons, wizards. Then we discovered science, and all the magic turned out to be atmospheric phenomena, weird mushrooms, and schizophrenia. Everything made sense, now that the world had rules to follow.

Sometimes I think back on those days, back when everyone still believed in the rules.

The world certainly didn't believe in them, that's for sure. They had lasted right up into the 21st century, when people believed that pretty much everything had been explained, and the only way to find anything really new was to get a doctorate and some superconducting magnets and start bashing particles together. The world allowed this sort of thing to go on for a few years, and then it got tired of the joke and went and changed on us.

December 3, 2013 was the day it all started, the day that magic revealed itself to the whole world. The date always made me chuckle; all the apocalyptic predictions were only a year off. Some people thought it was some kind of terrorist plot at first, and it certainly looked that way in some places: an entire herd of sheep in Australia exploded where they stood, and the Eiffel Tower rusted almost to pieces in front of thousands of people.

Some parts of it were less destructive, though: the Seattle Space Needle turned fluorescent green, St. Basil's Cathedral in Moscow vanished into thin air and reappeared the wrong way round, and a small town in Indiana doubled in population as every inhabitant suddenly turned into twins.

It turned out that all the weird things that had happened were just the tip of the iceberg, a glimpse into a world that had kept itself out of the public eye for centuries. Everyone in that hidden world had been happy to suppress and restrain their culture and keep us ordinary people ignorant and blissful, but then the bubble had burst. All that occult pressure could only be held back for so long. Thousands of people around the world were suddenly revealed as wizards, fairy creatures, and spirit whisperers, much to the surprise of their friends and employers, and in some cases, family members. For better or worse, we knew about them now, and we were all going to have to deal with it together.

There was a little panic and confusion at first, but after a couple of years what had once been strange and unreal had become just another kind of normal. Some people, both supernatural and not, tried to ignore the changes, and they had a rough time of it. Some people rode the crest of the wave, and they were ultimately better off, able to deal with both the mundane and the occult with equal ease. Fortunately, I was in the latter category.

My name is Frank Sylvester. I make my living as a private investigator. It's really not as glamorous a profession as the mystery novels would have you believe; most of us get hired to sneak around and catch people cheating on their spouses, or else we work for big companies to investigate potential investment opportunities. I always preferred my independence, which meant I had to do without a corporate safety net, so the magical revolution was a positive boon for my work. I wasted no time learning how magic worked and where its practitioners hung out, expanding my contact base to include as many different facets of supernatural culture as possible. I didn't let the strangeness bother me; on the contrary, I immersed myself in the strangeness up to my eyebrows. I was a professional investigator, after all, and here was something that clearly needed investigating. When people stopped panicking about magic and started asking questions about it, occult experts were going to be at a premium, so I set out to become an expert.

That was where I sat, with my thick contact list and my updated ad in the phone book, when I got a call from the governor's office asking me to come down to the capitol for a consultation. I quickly locked up my office and ran out to my old sedan, and I made my way downtown. I drove up to the parking garage and stopped at the security booth, where the guard checked my name against a list and handed me a parking pass. I pulled into a spot near the door and hung the pass on my mirror, and I strode into the building, trying not to look too nervous.

After asking for directions once or twice, I finally made my way to the Office of the Governor. It was the kind of office that merited the capital letters. The floor was covered with thick carpet, and all the chairs were cushioned in soft leather. I made a mental note to buy some new furniture for my office if this job panned out; the chair in front of my desk always made people want to get up and leave after a few minutes, which wasn't very good for repeat business.

I gave my name to the receptionist and took a seat in one of the delectably cushioned chairs, and I was quickly ushered into a side office with a crowded desk helmed by a young man in a loosened tie. "Frank Sylvester?" he asked.

"That's me," I said.

"It's a pleasure to meet you," he said as we shook hands.

"Bill Vance. I'm the governor's campaign manager. Can I get you a coffee, pastry?"

"No, thanks," I said.

"Well, Mr. Sylvester," he said, "let me get right to the point. We have received a threatening letter with the potential to damage the governor's upcoming reelection campaign. This threat seems to be of an occult nature. We need an expert in the supernatural who knows how to be discreet, and according to your ad, you're the best one in town."

"Mr. Vance, you flatter me."

"Normally, we wouldn't hire someone who didn't have some kind of track record," he said, "but it seems that such people are in short supply where the occult is concerned. Besides, a more... prominent investigator might cast an unwelcome spotlight on our situation, and as I said, we need this done discreetly. You can be discreet, can't you?"

"Of course," I said. "It's part of the job."

"Good. Do you accept?"

"Certainly. May I see the letter?"

He handed me a folded piece of typing paper. It was addressed to the governor in person and read:

> We have evidence in our possession that connects your office with an occult-oriented individual, which can be used to demonstrate that this individual exerts an illicit control over your actions as governor. As you know, such an influence would render one unfit for public office. If this evidence were made public, you would never again be able to serve the people of this state in any means whatsoever. For the moment, we will keep this evidence to ourselves, but in the fullness of time, we will make our

terms known to you so that the present state
of affairs can continue. Remember, be good to
your friends, and they will be good to you.

Well, this wasn't good. Ever since the change, one of
the things that got people the most nervous about magic was
the idea of mind control. It had taken a concerted effort from
the supernatural community to convince people how hard it
was to pull off. People learned how to protect themselves from
that kind of invasion as fervently as from unwanted pregnancy,
and people in important positions often took extra precautions.
An accusation that a public official was under magical compulsion was a serious charge. If it were true, the governor's career
would be over, as surely as if he'd gotten drunk and run his car
into a tree.

I paid particular attention to the line about being good
to your friends. If the governor had some kind of history that
was coming back to bite him, his campaign manager should
have been in the loop about it. This would require delicate
handling.

"I don't suppose you've had him tested for external
compulsion?" I said.

"Of course we have, under the table," Bill said. "He
checked out fine."

"What about a more mundane influence?" I said. "Do
you know if the governor is taking marching orders from anyone?"

"He says that he isn't, and I believe him," he said. "The
governor's a good man. He wouldn't do that kind of thing."
So either the governor hadn't told his own campaign manager
about his dirty past, which was a rookie move, or he was genuinely clean. This was getting complicated.

"Are there any other members of the governor's staff

with occult connections?"

"Not that I know of."

"All right, then. I'll need a list of names of everyone on the governor's staff, and I'll need a retainer."

"Certainly. The secretary will be able to give you the list, and I'll be right there with your check."

I spent the next couple of weeks following the governor's staffers around on the state's dime. I took pictures of them with a zoom lens and recorded a few phone conversations. I even brought along a gadget that a buddy of mine had made out of a laser microphone, an optical spectrometer, and about a dozen mood rings. He had this weird theory that the stuff in the mood ring had been developed in some secret government project back in the '60s to detect supernatural auras, so he had taken the stones from a bunch of mood rings and melted them down into some kind of filter. All I had to do, he said, was point the laser at a person, and the readout would tell me which side of the table they were on. It seemed like a long shot to me, but it wouldn't have been the first time he'd been right.

Eventually, I found myself camped outside the home of the governor's aide, having ruled out everyone above her on the totem pole. So far, everyone had come up as a normal human when I pointed the laser thingy at them. I was starting to think that my buddy was screwing with me. I watched the aide getting her things together for work in the morning as another woman entered the front room of their house holding a bicycle helmet. With the long-range mike, I heard them wish each other a good day at work, and then the aide kissed the other woman goodbye and headed into the garage.

The kiss took me a little by surprise, but not too much. People didn't bother so much anymore about non-traditional relationships when it was so much more interesting to bother about non-traditional physics. I waited until the aide's partner finished breakfast and headed out to the garage, and I pointed the laser thingy at her.

According to the readout, this woman was a wizard. I took another look at her through my binoculars. Out of all the kinds of people in the occult world, wizards were the hardest ones to pick out, but there were lots of subtle little hints that you learned to recognize, like how a police officer can tell if a person is concealing a weapon by the way they walk. I looked around the garage and saw how all the shelves and things were laid out, and then I watched her mount her bike and ride off, and I was certain that she was a wizard.

What do you know. The thingy actually worked.

I waited until she'd gotten far enough away that I could follow her without drawing attention. I managed to stay off her radar until she arrived at the library. She locked up her bike, and I followed her inside. I browsed around a few shelves until I caught a glimpse of her. She had changed from her biking clothes into something more librarian-y with a nametag, and she was pushing a hand cart full of books up and down the aisles.

"Excuse me . . . Judy?" I said, looking at her nametag.

"Yes? Can I help you?"

I showed her my PI license. "My name is Frank Sylvester. I'm a private investigator. I'd like to ask you some questions if I could."

"Of course." She wheeled her cart over to a table and pulled out a chair. I took a seat across from her and thought about how to phrase my first question as delicately as I could.

"I'd like to talk to you about your connection with the governor's office."

As soon as she heard the word "governor," her eyes widened and she started to get up, but I grabbed her wrist, not so hard as to leave a bruise but hard enough to keep her from running. I'm no bodybuilder, but I'm still a fairly big guy, and she couldn't have been more than a buck twenty. She wasn't going to get out of this without a struggle, and neither of us wanted to start a ruckus in a library.

"Please, it's all right," I said.

"Oh, God, I'm sorry, I didn't have a choice, he said –"

"Who? Who said?"

"I . . . I don't want . . ." She looked terrified.

"Please, I don't want to get you in trouble, but I need to know who sent the letter to the governor's office."

"I didn't have a choice," she said. "He said he'd hurt Katie if I didn't help him."

"Who?" I repeated. "Give me a name."

She hesitated for a while before speaking. "Sidney Chalk."

Ah. That would explain her hesitation. Sidney Chalk was a notorious crime lord in the local occult underground. He had fingers in pies all over town, from drugs to extortion to pit fighting. He was also a spirit whisperer, able to speak with and influence the dead. Rumor was that anyone who killed a member of his gang would be hunted down by their ghost.

Sidney Chalk getting his hooks into the governor was all kinds of bad news. With that kind of leverage, he could expand his operation over the whole state. The last thing I wanted to do was go toe to toe with him, but like Bill Vance had said, the governor was a good man. Of the two of them, I knew whose side I was on.

"Okay, Judy," I said. "I'm going to do everything I can to get you and Katie out of this, all right?"

"What are you going to do?" she said. "People have tried to hex him, you know. He's got protection."

"I'm sure he does," I said. "I'll just have to be smarter

than him."

I let Judy get back to her job, and I drove back downtown to the business district. I put some change into a meter and approached the headquarters of the Circle of Light, an advocacy group for disenfranchised persons of the occult persuasion. There were dozens of groups like this all over the country, but this was the only one in town that was a front for criminal activity. This was the center of Sidney Chalk's web, and everyone knew it. Finding him wasn't the problem.

I stepped into the main office and took a look around, and I could almost feel the air heating up around me from all the glares. I didn't have to be a keen observer of occult mannerisms to know that I was the only non-supernatural in the room, and I found myself suddenly wishing that I belonged to a minority group. My Scots/Irish/English/Swedish heritage hadn't exactly taught me how to relate with persecution, only how to consume beer and greasy food in large quantities. I couldn't exactly see anyone wearing a beige ribbon to promote Northern European Mongrel Awareness.

I scanned the room looking for any overt threats. The big guy looming by the back wall looked like any normal dude you might see at the gym, until you noticed his unusually thick mane of hair and the way his mouth seemed to protrude a little too far from his face. The little guy sitting on a bench was someone I recognized, a wizard with a green thumb and a hair-trigger temper, rumored to be one of Chalk's specialists. Rumor had it that several families out in the boonies had sold their land to Chalk cheap and moved away after it had become mysteriously overgrown with brambles. The other familiar figure was typing away at a desk. He wasn't the fastest of typists, which made sense, given that he appeared to be made entirely of stone.

I walked up to the reception desk and took a seat. The bored-looking clerk looked up from his paperwork and looked at me as though I had just broken wind in his face.

"Can I help you?"

"Yes, I have a question. If I wanted to send a letter to the governor asking him for a favor, who would I talk to about that? Is there a form I should fill out?"

The rest of the office went quiet. The straightforward approach had seemed like the best solution when I walked in, but now I wasn't so sure.

"I think you have the wrong office, sir," said the clerk.

"No, I don't think so. I could have sworn this was the place to go if I wanted to get a favor from the governor."

"Sir, I think you should leave."

"No, it's all right, James," said a woman from a door at the opposite end of the room. I stopped badgering the clerk and looked up at her. She would have turned heads in any bar in town. She also had feathers instead of hair and a fine coating of down over her arms, legs, and face, but maybe some people went for that kind of thing. "Please come in, Mr. Sylvester. Mr. Chalk would like to see you."

Well, that sent a chill up my spine. I started to think that this was a stupid plan. I must have been crazy to have just walked into Sidney Chalk's office like that. Sure, it wasn't likely that he'd just casually whack me where I sat, but still. The man knew my name, and here I was, coming in off the street to tweak his nose. The prospect of a hefty check from the governor must have fouled my judgment.

I walked into the rear office and sat down, face to face with Sidney Chalk. He didn't look like my idea of an occult mob boss, in his sweater vest and neat little glasses, but the way his eyes looked right through my head and out the other side told me everything I needed to know about him. This guy had chewed up and spat out a hundred guys like me in his time, and the magical revolution had only made his life easier, since now he could offer his services to anyone he wanted without having to disguise them. The only light spot in this meeting was that Sidney Chalk's guest chair was even more comfortable than the governor's.

"Frank Sylvester," he said. "So the governor got my little note, did he?"

"Yes, he did," I said. "He hired me to get to the bottom of it."

"Well, then, you've come to the right man," he said.

"I'm sorry?"

"You wanted to know who to talk to if you wanted to get a favor from the governor. After the election, I will be that man, Mr. Sylvester."

"I don't understand," I said. "You said you had evidence that the governor's office was connected to an occult individual, and I'm pretty sure I know who that is, but I don't see how that person could be controlling the governor."

"Oh, no, the aide's girlfriend is just a decoy," he said. "She's not really controlling him. She's just a leash to keep the governor in line. If he doesn't play ball, I have a few expendable enterprises I can hang around her neck. Voila, an evil sorceress who's been controlling the governor by way of her enthralled lover. And then, of course, there's his campaign funding."

"What do you mean?"

"Mr. Sylvester, I've had the governor in my pocket from day one," he said. "He ran for office on a strong pro-occult platform, and he needed support from advocacy groups like mine. And when you take into account all the other companies I control that donated to his campaign, why, it turns out that I'm his number-one supporter."

"Whew. And here I thought you were trying to smear the governor and make him look corrupt," I said.

"Indeed, Mr. Sylvester," he said. "He is already corrupt.

All I have to do is say so, and he is finished."

"I have one question, though, Mr. Chalk."

"Ask, by all means."

"Why are you telling me all this?" I really hoped that it wasn't because he was planning to kill me regardless.

"Well, I had planned to write another letter to the governor detailing my terms once his campaign started in earnest," he said, "but now that you're here, I might as well let you inform him of the situation yourself. I think it will be so much more meaningful coming from you, his trusted hireling."

"I'm touched," I said, as sarcastically as I dared.

"You will go back to your corrupt governor and tell him what I have told you," he said. "You will tell him that he has two options. If he accepts my offer, I will ensure that he is reelected, with all the funding that he desires to make our state a haven for all stripes, as long as he chooses to maintain our relationship. If he refuses, well, he is already a corrupt governor. I can always see to it that he becomes a corrupt ex-governor."

Right on cue, his fine, feathered secretary opened the door and showed me out. I walked steadily to my car and sat in the driver's seat, where I sat for five minutes as I allowed my hands to shake. I had never spent so much time in the company of a spirit whisperer before, and never one as dangerous as Sidney Chalk. I got the feeling that the next time I turned up in his path, he wouldn't be nearly as civil.

Once my nerves were back under control, I drove back to the capitol building and had a meeting with the governor, with Bill the campaign manager and Katie the aide. I told them the whole story. Bill needed to know all about the problem so he could perform proper damage control if necessary, and Katie needed to know about the trouble her partner would be in if things went south.

"This is terrible," said the governor. "Bill, I had no idea

that those contributions were coming from people like that, I swear."

"There was no way you could have known, sir," I said. "Sidney Chalk has friends all over town, probably all over the state. He knows that most people still don't understand the occult world very well."

"Is there anything we can do?" said the governor. "Can we find new donors?"

"Not this late in the game," said Bill. "Besides, it would look bad to turn down a donation from an occult advocacy group, and it would look even worse to accuse them of blackmail."

Suddenly, I had an idea. It was completely insane, and it would probably get me killed, but it was the only way to get the governor clear of Sidney Chalk's influence while keeping his reputation intact. While the governor and his campaign manager discussed strategy, I racked my brain for any other ideas that might offer less danger to life and limb, but nothing came.

They said that in the world of the occult, life was a little more intense, a little more exciting. In a world of grays and browns, the supernatural community was painted in vivid color. Nobody was wishy-washy about anything. Nobody did anything only a little bit. You stood up proud until you got knocked down. Well, if I was going to walk in that world, it was high time for me to start standing proud.

"Governor, I've thought of a way that you might get clear of this."

"What? What is it?" they all clamored.

"I can't tell you what I have planned. The only way this can work is if you aren't involved. When the dust settles, you have to be able to say that you didn't know anything about it. In fact, you need to forget that I was ever here today. We didn't meet, and you've never heard of Sidney Chalk."

"What are you talking about?" said Bill.

"Right now, only the four of us know anything about Sidney Chalk's connection to this office," I said. "That information must go no further than this room. You need to tell the press when this is over that you didn't know about Sidney Chalk's donations to your campaign. Can you do that?"

"Yes, I can," said the governor. "If you hadn't told me, I would never have suspected a thing."

"Good. Now, there's one more thing I'm going to need from you."

"Name it."

"I need to be able to offer somebody the promise of a pardon."

"What?" said Bill.

"I can't tell you any more than that. Do you trust me enough to let me offer someone a pardon in your name?"

The governor conferred with his campaign manager for a moment, and then he said, "Yes, Mr. Sylvester. I trust you."

"Good. Hopefully, I'll be sending you my bill tomorrow." I walked out of the office and went back to my car to take my fate in my hands.

I headed toward the park, where there was a nice little café nestled in among some trees. I had hoped to confirm a rumor, and sure enough, at a table on the patio sipping tea, I saw the green-thumbed wizard from Chalk's office. My plan was to exploit his short temper to my advantage, which unfortunately meant that I would have to put myself in danger. Well, apparently this was a day for me to endanger myself. I walked boldly over to his table and stood over him.

"Hey, pal, you're sitting in my seat."

"There are plenty of tables. Take any one you want," he said.

"Fine," I said, raising my voice, "I'll take this one. Get up."

"I don't want to get up," he said. I could already hear him making an effort to restrain his temper. "Please find a different table."

"You find a different table," I said, and I knocked the teacup out of his hand.

He looked down at the spilled tea, and he took a deep breath. Good. He was about to lose his temper. My plan to piss off a wizard was going swimmingly.

"You owe me a tea," he said.

"'I owe you a tea,'" I sneered back at him. "You still owe me a table, pipsqueak."

"Look, I'm trying to remain calm. Please don't make me angry."

"Oh, what, you're the Hulk now? What are you gonna do, pipsqueak?"

He looked me in the eye and made a gesture with his hand, and a branch from a nearby tree bent down and slapped me in the face.

"Oh, the little man's a wizard!" I crowed, getting more into the tough guy bully persona. "You gonna do some magic for me, little wizard?" I grabbed an iced coffee from a passing tray, and I threw it in his face.

"You want to see me do some magic?" he said, nearly vibrating with anger. "Fine!"

He thrust out his arm, and another branch slammed into me. This time, it knocked me off my feet, and I tumbled onto the grass. He then gestured at me with his other hand, and a full-grown tree sprang from the ground beneath me, entangling me in its branches. I bounced from limb to limb, eventually plummeting to the ground. I could barely move for bruises, but I still needed more.

"Come on, is that the best you can do?" I shouted, sway-ing a little for effect.

"Oh, you want the best I can do?" he screamed. "Have some more trees!" He gestured again, and more trees shot from the ground. I dodged as best I could, and I barely avoided getting impaled. I jumped from side to side, narrowly missing the foliage that the maniac was conjuring beneath me. "More trees!" he shouted. "Healthy trees! Happy trees! Can you smell what Bob Ross is cooking?"

By now, the café was in an uproar. Customers and wait-ers were running in a panic. I ran between the tables looking for cover, but trees were bursting up through the pavement now. The café's front window had been smashed by debris, and the canopy over the porch was in tatters. I ran for my life as the little wizard chased me, bringing the entire forest with him. When my legs could no longer carry me, I collapsed to the ground, and as he stood over me with murder in his eyes, a beanbag hit him square in the chest.

I turned to see a cadre of policemen armed with riot gear. They pelted the little wizard with beanbags and rubber bullets, and he went down like a sack of flour. As soon as he hit the ground, more officers blindfolded him, put him in hand-cuffs, and put mitts on his hands, which inflated and stiffened to keep him from casting. I blended in to the other onlookers and fleeing civilians as I watched the little wizard get hauled off to jail.

Later that afternoon, I stopped by the police precinct and asked to speak with the perpetrator. He had a court-ap-pointed lawyer with him, which was all for the better.

"You bastard," he said as soon as I sat down. "This is your fault."

"Relax, friend," I said.

"Relax?" he said. I checked to make sure he still had the

mitts on. "They've got me on destruction of public property, reckless endangerment, and who knows what else? I've got nothing to say to you that won't come out in court."

"I wouldn't worry about that if I were you," I said. "I'm here to make you an offer."

"No, I'll make you an offer," he said, lowering his voice. "You know who I work for, and when he hears about this . . ."

"Of course I know who you work for," I said. "That's why I'm here."

"What are you talking about, Sylvester?"

"I'm here to get you to testify against Sidney Chalk."

He stared at me. "You're either a moron, or you're crazy."

"Mr. Chalk is trying to get the governor in his pocket. You can put a stop to it, all by yourself. All you have to do is testify against him in court and get him put away for a long, long time for all the things we both know he's done. If you do that, I'm sure I can persuade the governor to offer you clemency."

"You can do all that?"

"Well, he did hire me to investigate the matter, and I haven't sent him my bill yet. I promise you that if you do this, I will do my utmost to see that you are rewarded for it."

"And what if I don't?"

"Then you'll get put away yourself."

"Bull. My boss will–"

"Your boss won't lift a finger to help you. If he were going to do anything for you, he would have hired you a fancy high-priced lawyer, but here you are, relying on a public defender. I can't see him going out of his way to support such a live wire as yourself, anyway. If I were in his shoes, I'd see you as a liability, a loose cannon. On the other hand, if you roll on him, you've got a chance at a fresh start. Maybe get yourself a place out in the country, far away from all this concrete and steel.

Someplace you might find yourself some serenity."

"I'd need to get far away from the city if I rolled on Chalk," he said, but I could tell the idea appealed to him. A tree-hugger like him didn't belong in a city. He needed to be able to see green out his window.

"Well, I'm sure you know people who can help you disappear," I said. "There must be a few wizards in this state that Sidney Chalk hasn't bent over his knee."

He didn't have a retort that time. He just sat there, thinking.

"Tell you what," I said. "You consider my offer, and I'll keep an eye on the proceedings. If you hold up your end of the deal, I'll hold up mine." I stood up from the table and walked to the door. "I'll see you around, pal."

"Not if I can help it, Frank," he said.

I turned and walked out of the precinct. There was an icepack and a bottle of ibuprofen back home with my name on it.

Two weeks later, I saw on the news that Sidney Chalk had been implicated in a heinous series of crimes throughout the state. The report said that Mr. Chalk's conviction was assured by the testimony of an anonymous former employee of his, who had been rewarded for his assistance with a full pardon from the governor and transportation to an undisclosed location. In a speech, the governor applauded the courage of the unnamed informant, and he expressed his wish that the entire occult community could follow this man's example and help the police bring supernatural criminals like Sidney Chalk to justice. I noticed that there was no mention at all of any potential irregularities with the governor's fundraising efforts. Bill Vance must have been a good man to have around the office.

I switched off the TV and looked at the framed commendation on my wall, thanking me on behalf of the governor for my exemplary service to the state. With such a testimonial as that, as well as the positive word of mouth I could expect in the occult community from my involvement with this case, I looked forward to many new clients, who could rest easy in my brand-new, well-padded guest chair.

ALL THE HUSH-HUSH AT THE FARMHOUSE

Amanda Dorman

Unfortunately, I am an only child.

If I weren't an only child I would've been at journalism camp with the other guys. Not at this crappy farm.

I hadn't even gotten out of the car and already I could smell the putrid odor of healthy plants and even healthier animals, though it definitely did not smell healthy.

See if I had a brother, I could've just made him come instead. Robert and Ana didn't really care about me; they just needed a kid to prove that we're functional. It didn't matter who it is. If I had a brother, they could choose. Or better yet, a sister. Everybody loves girls.

I looked dejectedly out the window. A huge, hand-made banner was hung over the large red barn. It was really just a white bed sheet with the words "Greenmann-Jones Family Reunion" painted in large red letters. The paint was still wet and the red was dripping. It reminded me of history class. In like the Middle Ages or something, they would hang the marital bed sheet up in public after the wedding night so everyone could make sure the bride was a virgin. Gross.

"Christopher Bobby Jones!" Ana yelled at me, "Get out of the car and help with the bags!"

I sighed and opened the car door. Hot, dusty air

invaded my face. I wheezed and grabbed at my pockets for my inhaler.

"Topher! Your mother told you to get the bags," Robert yelled from somewhere unseen.

I fumbled my inhaler into my mouth and searched the wide landscape for my parents while I tried not to die. It seemed I was allergic to just about everything in this god-forsaken place. Not to mention the asthma.

There was literally nothing worth existing here. All I could see was the barn, a few parked cars, and miles of corn fields.

"Topher!"

I whipped my head to the right. In the distance sat a large farmhouse. I saw my mother moseying towards it. My father, on the other hand, was sprinting in my direction. There was another man matching his pace, it was my Uncle John. I slammed the car door, pocketed my inhaler, and headed towards the already open trunk.

"Come on son," Robert said, reaching me in no time. He wasn't even out of breath, "Let's get a move on."

"Give the kid a break," said Uncle John.

"Uncle John!" I smiled and held out my fist, which was promptly bumped. Uncle John was the only one here that got that. He was only thirty-two and already he was a US senator. And he wasn't stupid enough to get married either. My father was forty, married, and still in local government. But we don't really talk about that.

"Hey kid," Uncle John said, punching me in the shoulder. Pain radiated through me as he hit the bone. I tried not to wince.

"Why don't you feed this kid, Robert? He looks like he'll blow away any second," Uncle John asked. He walked behind the car to join my father. I followed.

The trunk held my backpack, a small duffel for Robert, and two large leopard print suitcases that were Ana's. Great.

I grabbed the duffel and my backpack before Robert had a chance to tell me what to take and started for the house. He didn't say anything, but I could feel his disapproving glare on my back.

Uncle John caught up to me quickly, one of Ana's suitcases in hand.

"So Toph, what have you been up to?" he asked me.

I heard the trunk slam and the locks click into place behind us.

"Not much," I said.

"Come on!" Robert said, his footsteps crunched the dirt road louder as they got closer, "I'll race you!"

Robert took off, passing me quickly and not looking back. The heavy suitcase thumped against his side, but he didn't even notice. Uncle John hurried to catch up to him. His booming laugh echoed back to me.

I didn't even try to beat them. Hay fever sucks no matter what, but when you add actual hay into the mix, well, I definitely was not going to be running any time in the next week.

I could see a clump of the men standing over at the edge of one of the corn fields. Even from far away I could tell who was who. The Joneses were all wearing jean shorts. The Greenmanns and Goldbergs were all wearing yacht gear, even though we were seriously land-locked here. Aunt Margaret always made her family match, so the Goldbergs were all wearing yellow today. There was also some guy in a dark sweatshirt. That was weird, but I couldn't tell who it was from so far away.

The farm house was one of those old ones that survived the civil war. It contained at least ten bedrooms and featured a large porch that wrapped all the way around the house. Dozens of rocking chairs were scattered around it. A good number of them were occupied already.

Dominating the porch was a large clump of women, rocking their chairs furiously and using random objects as fans. This was my mother's family, the Jews.

Fat Aunt Margaret was hard to miss. She was wearing a bright yellow dress. My mother sat beside her, catching up on sister stuff I guess.

I wish I had a sister.

My cousin Liza was sitting there too, looking incredibly bored. Cell phones didn't work out here. Liza was really pretty. She was probably missing hundreds of calls from boys at her school.

Aunt Margaret's daughter, Bella-May sat next to Liza. As I walked closer I heard Bella-May's shrill shrieks of excitement as she tried to get Liza to talk to her. But Bella-May is only 6, so Liza wasn't listening.

Nana Jones was also there with her daughter, my Aunt Maria. They were leaning over Aunt Sylvia's lap. Aunt Margaret and my mother were also paying Sylvia's lap a lot of attention, which was weird because usually they tried to ice out Aunt Sylvia, who had made the mistake of marrying their favorite brother, Bobby.

I heard a shriek come from under the elevated porch. A clump of dirt with long blond hair shot out towards me.

It was Jackie. I guess she's technically my aunt, since she's my dad's sister. But she's only nine. So mostly she's just annoying.

I braced myself as Jackie collided into me. A cloud of dirt puffed up from her no longer white T-shirt, and I started wheezing again. Jackie wrapped her arms around me and squeezed. I think I stopped breathing entirely. I fumbled for my inhaler.

"I am sooooooo glad you're here!" Jackie squealed. She grabbed my hand, the one holding the inhaler, and yanked me up the porch steps. I gasped for breath as I stumbled after her. We reached the top and she let me yank my hand free. I dropped Robert's duffle bag and used both hands to cling to the inhaler rushing life-saving medicine into my lungs.

Suddenly I was surrounded by chattering women.

"Asthma."

"Such a pity."

"Not even good at math either."

"I worry about him. So sickly."

"And to think he is the only one of our kids tall enough for sports," that one was Aunt Margaret, talking to my mother. They had all gotten up and were slowly invading my personal bubble.

"What about Allen?" Aunt Sylvia's voice rang out. I couldn't see her though. The throng of women was too thick to see anything past the first lines.

"He's too short," they all said.

"He's not short, he's fun-sized," Aunt Sylvia shot back. Nobody laughed.

"He only does that basketball to make me worry, you know," Aunt Margaret complained.

"He could get seriously hurt"

"But at least he's not sickly like Topher here," that one was my own mother.

They were closing in, if I was gonna make it out alive, I had to escape now. I tried to side-step in between Nana Jones and Aunt Maria, and ran straight into Aunt Sylvia.

Well I almost did, something stopped me a few inches from her face. I looked down to see what it was, and jumped back in alarm. My eyes widened. I pointed and stammered, "P-p-pregnant!" It was all I could think to say. I felt the heat of blood rush to my cheeks.

"I know. Gross right? I think they did it on my bed," Liza rolled her eyes at me. She hadn't moved from the chair.

"Liza!" my mother exclaimed. They turned away from me and towards her as if they were all sharing some master brain. That comment started a whole new disapproving rant that, thankfully, didn't include me. I grabbed Robert's duffle and made my escape.

On my way to the front door I passed Grandpa Bob. He was sitting there, alone, muttering to himself. Grandpa Bob never really recovered after Grandma Alison died a few years ago.

"Hey! Hey! You! Boy!" Grandpa Bob grabbed my T-shirt and I was once again trapped.

"Hey Grandpa Bob," I said reluctantly.

"Don't tell your Grandmother now, but I let Bobby sneak a little booze. Just let her keep thinking it's that inner-ear condition, though." Grandpa Bob pulled my shirt in closer until my nose was touching his. His breath smelled like tomatoes. I leaned away and tried to loosen his grip.

"Ok Grandpa Bob," I said.

He pulled me in once more, "Promise!"

I held up my hands in surrender, "I promise," I sighed.

"Good," Grandpa Bob let go of me and patted my now wrinkled shirt. His hand was almost bigger than my whole stomach.

I retreated into the house as fast as I could. I dumped

my backpack and Robert's duffle next to my mother's stuff in the living room and headed to the kitchen. Grandpa Jones had made a pitcher of his lemonade. Finally, something good about this place.

I poured myself a large glass, not caring that I was emptying the pitcher, and plopped down at the table. The drone from the porch was less intrusive in here. My glass dripped cold condensation all over my hand. I sighed happily and took a deep gulp.

My throat burned as it went down. I coughed, banging myself on the chest as I struggled for air. Uncle Stephen had gotten to the lemonade; it was spiked with rum or something. The Greenmanns were not gonna like that.

I looked out the window, the women were still yammering on. And no one else was around. I checked behind me and everything, just to make sure. Then I smiled and took another sip, smaller this time. I pretended like it didn't burn my insides.

"So whatcha wanna do?" Jackie's voice came from behind me.

I jumped and the glass slipped. I caught it just in time.

"Whoa! Did you see that! I snatched it out of thin air! That was awesome!" I said proudly.

"Yeah, cool," Jackie replied, unimpressed, "So watcha wanna do?"

I sighed and set down my drink, wiping my cold wet hands on my jeans, "There is nothing to do Jackie. There is never anything to do at these stupid things. Nothing ever happens. So just go away."

"Yeah-huh," Jackie said, plopping down in the chair next to me, "Stuff always happens. We're just not supposed to talk about it. Can I have some?" Jackie reached for my glass.

I grabbed the lemonade in alarm and hunched over it in protection, "Uh, no," I tried to change the subject, "What do you mean? We're not supposed to talk about what?"

Jackie stuck out her tongue at me, "Meanie! You're supposed to share with me. Your mom said so. I'll tell!" Jackie stood up.

"Wait!," I reached out to stop her, "How about a soda?"

Jackie put her finger to her chin like she was thinking hard. She tossed her hair and I leaned away from the dust cloud.

"Okay," she said, "I want a Coke."

"You're not supposed to have caffeine..." I started. Jackie narrowed her eyes and I caved immediately, "Okay, okay, Coke it is."

I took my lemonade with me as I grabbed a Coke from the top shelf of the fridge. As I handed it to her, I guided her back to the table.

"What did you mean, we're not supposed to talk about it?" I asked.

I heard the *kkshhh* as Jackie opened the soda. She slurped at the can and looked up at me, "Well like one time I heard Uncle Stephen say that his wife has her own room, they don't even live together most of the time. But then everyone was all hush-hush and didn't want to talk about it."

"Huh," I slapped at a bug buzzing somewhere near my head, "That's sad."

"Yeah and another time I heard my brother Robert telling my daddy that your mommy had a histromecamy. And my daddy was like 'Don't talk so loud!'" Jackie took another slurp of the soda, "Do you know what a histmymomany is?"

"No," I lied. I didn't even want to know that my mother had had a hysterectomy, much less explain it to my nine year-old aunt.

"Oh. Well, it doesn't sound fun," Jackie said, staring at the table. She started drawing happy faces in the wood with her finger.

"Hmm," I said. I felt the tingling of an idea beginning to form.

"Or like with Mr. Bobby. Mrs. Margaret always hush-hushes Mrs. Sylvia when she talks about it." Jackie started using what little was left of her fingernails to draw on the table, leaving little scratches in the varnish. I couldn't hear any sound they were making, but it still hurt my ears somehow. The drawings caught the dancing light coming in from the window, making them almost look alive.

"What? Who?" I asked.

"What your grandpa was just talking about," Jackie said, "With Mrs. Sylvia's Bobby."

"Oh. Right. I call him Jerk Bob," I said.

Jackie burst out laughing. I scooted her soda away so she wouldn't knock it over. She was practically in tears.

"Cause, cause he's really mean!" Jackie said as she struggled to control her laughter, "I like it!"

"Just don't say it to any of the grownups," I said, smiling a little. Jackie fell out of her chair. I chuckled as she made a scene on the floor.

There are too many Bobs in my family. It started with like my Great-Great-Grandfather Robert. It goes all the way to Grandpa Bob, who named his eldest son Bobby, I call him Jerk Bob because I already used up all the other variations of Robert there were. Also because Jerk Bob is a jerk.

Uncle Bob is Aunt Margaret's Bob. She also has a baby son named Bob Ross Goldman. I think the idea was to call him Ross when he's older. But my mother and Aunt Margaret have a weird obsession with the name Bob, so I really don't think that's gonna happen. We just call him Bob Ross.

My father, at least, refuses to go by anything other than Robert, but I've heard Ana call him Bob behind his back. She wanted to name me Bob too. But Robert didn't faint in the birthing room, so he won the bet and I was Christopher instead. For a while she tried to tack on my middle name, and she called me Topher Bobby. But someone told her that sounded British, so she stopped.

Jackie was still on the floor. She was just laughing for attention now. But she had a point. And I had an idea. Even though at church every Sunday they're always saying don't gossip, my family was really, really good at it. Then again the Greenmanns were Jewish, so maybe it was okay for them. My mother is a Messianic Jew. That's another thing we "don't" talk about.

You know what? If I couldn't be at journalism camp, then I was gonna do my journalism right here. I grabbed my lemonade and left Jackie on the floor. I had some research to do.

That night, after dinner, I took my notepad and sat down next to Aunt Margaret. Ever since Grandma Alison had passed, Aunt Margaret was in charge. There wasn't anything going on here that she didn't know about.

"So, Aunt Margaret. What's up?" I asked.

Aunt Margaret raised her eyebrows and turned to Uncle Bob, "What is the matter with kids these days? Don't they teach English at schools anymore? What is this 'What's up?' and 'hollering at your brother' even if you don't have a brother? If I was in charge, oh, I'm telling you. It would be different."

"And we would all be better for it dear," Uncle Bob said, not looking up from the thick novel he was reading.

Aunt Margaret nodded, satisfied, and turned back to me, "Why don't you go practice basketball with my Allen over there"

She nodded fondly at her son in the other room. He had six cups arranged in a triangle at one end of the kitchen table, and was standing at the other end, practicing bouncing ping-pong balls into them.

Well that was a failure. Aunt Margaret was not even looking at me. She was leaning down to play with Bob Ross on the floor. Her dress gaped open at the top and I was suddenly grateful I wasn't sitting on the other side of the room.

"You're not doing it right," I looked to the other side of me and found Jackie. She had been forced to bathe, so she actually passed for human now.

"What do you mean?" I asked.

"You can't just ask her. She won't talk about it. You have to be sneaky. Have a excuse," Jackie explained, "Then it's easy."

"Well if it's so easy, why don't you do it?" I taunted.

"Fine," Jackie said. She went to stand in front of fat Aunt Margaret, "Mrs. Margaret?"

"Yes dear?" Aunt Margaret smiled sickeningly at her. Girls. Everybody likes them.

"Well I was just wondering. How come Mrs. Sylvia's tummy is so big now when Liza is practically a grown up and Mr. Bobby is so..." Jackie's voice dropped in volume and she leaned in close to Aunt Margaret, "...old?"

Aunt Margaret reached for her glass of lemonade sitting on the table in front of her, and took a big sip. She shook her head and gritted her teeth like it hurt to swallow, set the glass back, and leaned in close to Jackie.

"Well," she whispered, I leaned over in my chair, ears open, "You didn't hear this from me sweetie. But Mrs. Sylvia is not as old as Mr. Bobby, see. And some people say, not me of course, but some people," Aunt Margaret's voice got even quieter. I almost tipped my chair over trying to hear, "some people say that maybe Mr. Bobby didn't have anything to do with that tummy at all."

I tipped my chair, and fell all over someone's feet.

"Careful there kid," it was Uncle John.

He bent down and righted the chair, with me still in it.

I felt my face grow hot. I mumbled something about playing around. He didn't embarrass me by asking questions. Instead he drew the attention elsewhere.

"Whatchu reading there Bob?" Uncle John asked, stepping over Bella-May, who was playing on the floor.

"Book," Uncle Bob.

"Good to know, good to know," replied Uncle John good-naturedly. Suddenly he wrinkled his nose and turned to talk to Aunt Margaret.

"Whewie! Can you smell what Bob Ross is cooking there Margaret?" He waved his hand in front of his face as he asked.

It hit me then. I pulled my shirt over my mouth and nose, swallowing the bit of vomit in the back of my throat. It smelled like that time Jackie lied about checking for all the eggs in the chicken coop and I had to clean it after they had all been sitting there for a month. I gagged.

Aunt Margaret lifted Bob Ross up by the armpits and smacked his butt against her nose.

"Yup," she said, "it's about that time," she shoved Bob Ross into Uncle Bob's unsuspecting arms. He calmly balanced the baby whilst reluctantly shutting his book, "It's time for the kid's bedtime anyways. Come on Bella-May."

Aunt Margaret whisked Bella-May out of the room. Uncle Bob followed silently with the baby.

The absence of ping-pong noises and pseudo-manly grunts coming from the kitchen meant that Allen too had wandered off somewhere. The only ones left downstairs now were Uncle John, Jackie, and myself.

"You see?" Jackie said, slumping down on the couch smugly, "You just have to be sneaky."

"Ooo, sneaky about what?" Uncle John asked.

"Topher is gonna do his journalism about all the hush-hush in the house," Jackie replied.

"Jackie!" I protested. She ignored me.

"Huh. Persistent about this journalism thing are you? Well good for you kid," Uncle John said. He reached for the lemonade Aunt Margaret left on the coffee table and took a long swig.

Cool. I knew Uncle John would be cool.

"Thanks," I said, "So, uh, do you have any dirt for me?"

Uncle John put his feet on the coffee table and leaned back into the couch, holding the glass of lemonade, "Well the Greenmanns haven't really done anything special since we fled Austria in the Forties. Some of us died over there, you know. Damn Nazis."

"Yeah, I know," I said, a little disappointed.

We heard Uncle Stephen singing loudly and off-key outside on the porch.

"If I was a monkey's uncle! I'd saddle her tooooooooo!"

It was the song he always sang when he was drunkest.

Jackie giggled, "That song is funny."

"Yes, and a pretty girl like you should not listen," Uncle John said, "Wait," he turned to me; I could almost see a cartoon light bulb turn on over his head, "I know what you can do for your project. Go outside and talk to your Uncle Stephen. Ask him if he likes the last name Jones."

I pursed my lips in confusion, "Uh, okay."

"Yay! Let's go outside!" Jackie said, jumping up.

"Not so fast young lady. It's bedtime for you," Uncle John said.

"Awwww!" Jackie complained. She sat back down on the couch, arms folded across her chest.

"I'll tell you a bedtime story," Uncle John bargained.

"YES!" Jackie shouted. And she was on her feet and headed up the stairs, Uncle John following in her wake. He winked at me as he left the room. I smiled. Uncle John told the best stories.

I went outside. Uncle Stephen was standing behind an empty rocking chair, pushing it back and forth much faster than it was ever intended to go. He was alone in the dark, still singing to himself.

"Well hi-er ther! Ta-ta-ta-topher!" said Uncle Stephen, opening his mouth as wide as it would go as he stumbled over the first part of my name. He swung his arms up in greeting, the liquid sloshed around in the bottle he was holding. But there was so little left, it didn't spill out. The already out of control rocking chair clattered loudly to the ground.

"Whoops!" Uncle Stephen tried to bend over and pick it up. But he was having some trouble with balance. He grabbed a neighboring rocking chair to try to steady himself, but it didn't work very well. He almost took that one down too.

I stepped in; making sure Uncle Stephen was seated securely enough, before righting the overturned chair and sitting down myself.

"Hey Uncle Stephen," I said.

"Whoa! It's like the ocean!" Uncle Stephen rolled his head around violently and moved around in the chair, "Have you ever been to the ocean, uhhh?"

He was blanking on my name?

"Topher," I supplied the end of his sentence.

"Topher! Have you ever, everreallyever been to the ocean Topher?" Uncle Stephen rolled his head dramatically to look at me before taking a long swig of clear liquid from the bottle in his hand. He bobbed around, trying to stay seated. Why didn't we have any normal chairs out here?

"Yes," I said, "Uncle Stephen I have a question for you."

"Anything for my son!"

"Nephew."

"Even better," he pronounced every single syllable, stopping on the 'v' for a long time and squeezing his lips tight to make a popping 'b' sound.

"Yes. Um. Uncle Stephen, do you like your last name?"

He made a face like there was a horrible taste in his mouth. He scrunched up his eyes and stuck his tongue in and out of a wide-open mouth, like he was trying to get something off it.

"Ick! No!" he said, his head drooping forward suddenly. A warm night breeze bathed my faced and bolstered my courage.

"Why?" I asked.

"Cause it's not German!" Uncle Stephen's head snapped up, his eyes were fiery.

"We're German?" I raised my eyebrows at him, "Are you sure we're not Irish?"

"Bleh!" he shook his head and spit on the ground. He held the bottle over his head proudly, "This is vodka, boy. That's the Polish!" Uncle Stephen burst out laughing. It took a minute to calm him down. He was just doing it for the attention, "Pole! Ha!" He pointed at the wooden column supporting the porch over-hang and almost fell over again.

"Oh yeah, funny. That's a pole-ish," I said, "So we're Polish and German then?"

He stopped the laughing.

"Mostly German. That's the good stuff. Had a good German name too. Until we came here."

This was getting interesting.

"We changed our name?" I asked, "Why?"

"Cause it got tainted! That's why! Tainted!" Uncle Stephen almost fell out of his rocking chair again. I leaned forward to help him. It was too dark to really see his face, but he looked a little angry. I couldn't really tell though.

"What was it?" I was intrigued.

Uncle Stephen looked left and right. Two figures were standing way at the other end of the porch, under the porch light. It was Jerk Bob and another guy I didn't recognize. But they were too far away to hear anything if it was whispered.

Uncle Stephen leaned in close to me. He smelled like booze and vomit. Gross. I sucked it up, though, and leaned in with him.

"Our name was...Hitler," he whispered.

I was stunned. I was related to Hitler? Not *Adolf* Hitler, surely?

Uncle Stephen started squealing. He sounded a lot like Jackie.

"When your mom found out. Whoo-ee, she almost divorced my poe little brother man!"

"What?!" I exclaimed. I sat up straight, eyes wide. My parents almost got divorced? Over a name? How did I not know this?

"But then she found out he was laundering all that money through her account and if she left, she'd be on the hook for all of it!" He could barely contain his glee.

I was speechless. I... what? I didn't want to believe it. But I knew Uncle Stephen, and he was a lot of things, but a liar was not one of them. Not even a drunk liar.

"He-he-he-he!" Uncle Stephen fell out of his chair. I couldn't tell if he was laughing or struggling to breathe. The bottle fell out of his hand, the little remaining contents spilling on the ground. I bent down to check on him, putting my face real close to see if I could hear him breathing.

Suddenly he snored louder than when the rocking chair had fallen over. I felt the force of it pull a few strands of my hair towards his face. I jumped back in disgust. I ran my hands all through my hair and shook like a dog, trying to get rid of the drunk uncle smell.

I stepped over Uncle Stephen and sat down hard a few rocking chairs down. I sat down so fast, I almost tipped over backwards.

The Hitler thing was bad, yeah. But it was just a name. And it might not even be *that* Hitler. Mostly that was just weird. But money laundering?

I barely even knew what that was. And everything I did know I learned from T.V. so who knows if it was even accurate? It's not that I couldn't believe something like that of Robert. I mean he's not all bad. I wouldn't think he would murder someone or anything. But white collar crime, well I mean that wasn't too bad, was it? I could see him doing that.

"I already told you!" someone screamed. I looked up. Jerk Bob was yelling at the other guy at the end of the porch. Great. Another drunk uncle. I got up to go inside.

"Queer! A fuckin' queer!" yelled Jerk Bob.

I froze. Quietly I edged my way closer, sticking to the shadows.

"That doesn't matter. I need the other evidence you said you had," a man in a dark sweatshirt replied calmly to Jerk Bob. A piece of wood creaked within the house somewhere. Jerk Bob looked back in alarm.

"Of course it matters," he hissed, "A United States senator, a Republican, is *carrying on* right underneath our noses," Jerk Bob said, lowering his voice.

"You said you had something else," the sweatshirt man hissed back. He glared over Jerk Bob's shoulder, at a spot on the wall dangerously close to me. A cold breeze rushed over me and I shrank even further into the shadows, making myself as small as I could.

"Fine," Jerk Bob said, throwing up his hands, "If sins against God no longer matter... You want to hear about the girls?"

The man's eyes lit up.

"It's all Cortez's operation, you know. We just help get them through customs. Cover it up if one ever gets away. You're missing the big thing! There is a gay in our midst." Jerk Bob rubbed his hands together, intertwining them at random, while he talked.

"Illegally? They get past customs illegally?" the sweatshirt man whispered excitedly.

My throat started to close up on me. I pulled out my inhaler, trying not to hyperventilate as I tried to get oxygen into my lungs without being overheard.

"Yeah. By switching out the paperwork on the cargo." Jerk Bob said, not really interested in sweatshirt man anymore.

"And you've seen this?"

"Yeah. I had to help last Tuesday. One of the girls escaped," Jerk Bob looked up suddenly, "But I'm immune right? You said I was immune."

"Yes, yes," sweatshirt man said excitedly. Jerk Bob sagged with relief. Sweatshirt man turned to face the corn fields, "You got it?" he asked the air, "Is it enough?"

Suddenly floodlights filled the night sky. My hiding

place in the now shadow-less shadows was no longer safe. The lights blinded me and I covered my eyes as pain shot through them, I fell against the wall as a full on panic attack came at me full force.

Police sirens pierced the calm. I could hear what seemed like hundreds of boots running along the porch. Above it all I heard Bella-May's screaming. I forced myself to calm down, using my inhaler to steady my breathing. I gathered my courage and looked up. It took a few seconds for my eyes to adjust to the lights.

Slowly my vision returned to me. I saw people run out of the house. First there were about five police men, leading the way to a whole fleet of police vehicles sitting in front of the house. Then came a shrieking Aunt Margaret, clutching an even louder Bella-May.

"There are kids in the house!" shouted Uncle John's voice from inside the building.

Uncle Stephen stumbled past me, towards the crowd. I followed him in haste. My mom was screaming my name. I ran to her and she pulled me close. I embraced her back, trying to retain a small piece of the reality that was crashing down all around me.

Relatives swarmed around in confusion. I caught a glimpse of Jackie, hiding underneath the porch. Dogs were barking, Bob Ross was crying. Chickens were being trampled, their dying cries drowned out by the mayhem encompassing us all.

Another set of policemen came out of the house, this one led by a very proud-looking man in a dark sweatshirt. An armed guard, escorting a handcuffed prisoner, rushed towards the waiting police cars.

"Wait!" Uncle Stephen stumbled forward, "Wait! You can't take... that's my wife!" He fell over as he chased after the police men that were hauling my Aunt Maria bodily away in handcuffs. The police simply stepped around him, ignoring his presence all together. Out of the corner of my eye I saw Uncle John silently bend down and help him stand.

"You can't arrest me!" Aunt Maria proclaimed hotly, "I am a United States Senator! I represent this state in Washington D. C.! I have rights!"

"You have the right to remain silent," the sweatshirt man began as he forced Aunt Maria into to back of the police car. The smile on his face almost tore it in half.

I coughed and reached for my inhaler as the smog of the city invaded the car. My parents had been silent the entire trip back. We only had about an hour left before we were home.

"Well," my mother finally ventured, "Well." That was all she could say.

So I jumped in.

"Next year, I'm going to journalism camp," I said.

"We'll see," replied my mother, "we might just want to stick together. I've had enough dirty crime to last a lifetime."

"No," I said, "I am going to camp."

"If we have the money, Topher, then maybe," my father ventured, peering at me through the rearview mirror.

"Oh, we have the money. I know that for a fact. And it's not dirty either. It's very clean. Almost like you stuck it in the laundry," I said. I let my words echo in their heads, my voice saturated with meaning.

Robert slammed on the brakes and we all jerked forward.

"W-what did you say?" he asked. They both stared straight ahead, unmoving. Not even breathing. Cars honked and passed us, their drivers shouting obscenities. None of us paid them any attention. An icy stillness enveloped the car.

"You heard me," I replied stonily, "I am going to journalism camp."

Silently Robert pressed the accelerator and we started to move towards home again.

We were silent for the rest of the hour.

We were silent for the rest of the year.

THE HAWK

Kristy Tejeda

Chapter One

Gregory Jones was fat. Not extremely fat, mind you, but fat enough that he could grab a handful of extra padding around his middle and give it a good shake. His stomach jiggled and jumped as he shook it, the thick glossy brown fur covering his massive belly rippling in tiny waves.

Dismayed, Gregory plopped down into the kitchen chair and gave a great sigh. The cold season, where a mouse needs extra padding, had officially ended seven months ago. It was now mid-summer, the hottest days of the year drawing near, and Gregory still had the stubborn fat bulges of hibernation hanging around his midsection. All the other mice in Hollowed Wood were already lean and trim. It was just Gregory with his chunky frame who still hung on to those pesky extra ounces.

Maybe it was all those sweet dandelion clovers I ate, he thought to himself. But he knew it was a lie. It didn't matter if he gorged himself on wildflowers or went on a strictly acorns-only regime. The result was always the same. Every year the other mice in his town began to shed the winter weight. But Gregory stayed the same, fat as ever.

Maybe it's in my genes, he thought sarcastically. *I bet my great-grandmother was a squirrel.*

With a dismayed groan at his own pathetic joke, he heaved himself out of the chair and went to pour himself another cup of coffee. He used two whole espresso beans this time! *Might as well*, he thought glumly as he slowly sipped his drink.

While he thought about his plight he walked around the house removing all the tree-bark coverings from the tiny windows, opening them to let the morning sunlight stream through. Gregory took a deep breath, his whiskers twitching in delight.

Since a hawk had been preying on the area for the past few weeks the Mayor had ordered everyone to cover their windows in the evenings so the night-feeding bird wouldn't be able to detect where they lived.

"It's a precaution really," the Mayor had said at the last town hall meeting. "Hawks have a notoriously bad sense of smell. They are guided principally by their eyesight and will be greatly deterred if our whole village is blacked out. We've already lost too many of our citizens to this beast. I won't have us lose any more."

Gregory had put them up immediately. He really didn't want a hawk making an hors d'oeuvre out of him.

Or a main course, he thought grumpily, remembering all those extra ounces around his chunky midsection. He grabbed the roll of fat again, giving it a good shake. *I'll bet my great-grandfather was a squirrel.*

Chapter Two

"Three jacks and two sevens. That there is a full house, boys! Read 'em and weep!" Ed threw his cards down on the table with a flourish and greedily raked up the chips. The other players at the table groaned, knowing the game was done. Ed had come in at the end and swept it just like he always did.

Gregory was disappointed. He had gambled more acorns than he should have hoping to make up for last week's loss. Ed, his auburn furry ears wiggling in glee, poured all the winning acorns into his bag and sat back, laughing.

"I don't know what you're so happy about Ed," Gregory said, frowning at the chuckling mouse who talked like a back country rodent. "You win practically every week. It really shouldn't come as any sort of great shock."

Ed took a big swig of his elderberry beer. "Ah, lighten up Chubby," he said, giving Gregory an amused look. "Don't bet so many acorns next time if yous goin' to be such a sore loser."

"He's right," the Mayor interjected, straightening his top hat. "You take this game far too seriously, young man."

Gregory took a small sip of beer, sulking.

"Oh, let him be Mayor," Bob Ross offered, pushing his chair back from the table and lighting a cigarette. "The four of us get together every Wednesday to play a rowdy game of poker, not nag each other to death."

Gregory shot Bob a thankful look. As his best friend, Bob always had his back no matter how many times he got picked on. Besides, he really wasn't in the mood to be lectured to, especially not from the Mayor. That mouse could get so preachy sometimes! Gregory wondered why Bob even let the Mayor come to Wednesday poker nights. Occasionally the politician was good for a laugh, but rarely. The uptight mouse was so straight-laced that all his glossy black fur had to be combed in the same direction. Gregory wondered if the Mayor went over it every morning with a straight edged comb, meticulously checking every hair. And he never went anywhere without that stupid black top hat. Thankfully, he was up for re-election in the fall and would soon spend most of his time out campaigning instead of here at Bob's house on poker nights.

"So, which of you rodents are up for another game, eh?" Bob said, shuffling the cards on his knee, and puffing away at the cigarette.

"Sorry boys," the Mayor said, taking his last swig of beer and daintily wiping his mouth. "I told the Mrs. I would be home in time to put up the tree-bark blinds on the windows. Don't you fellows forget to do the same now, do you hear? Old Mr. Woodchuck told me he saw that darn hawk circling Hallowed Wood six times last night! We haven't had any casualties for a few nights now and I'd hate to break that spell." He gave the mice a genuinely friendly smile, which Gregory immediately took the wrong way, put on his black top hat, and left.

"Ah fooey," Gregory said, faking an attempt at disappointment. "I guess we don't have enough players now for another round."

Ed gave him a sideways smirk. "You ain't foolin' nobody with that fake field mouse sentimentality crap, Chubby. You ain't never liked the Mayor and might as well just say it."

"I like him just fine," Gregory lied. "He's just a little uppity is all."

"If you be askin' me, I be thinkin' yous the uppity one, Chubby," Ed countered.

Bob lit another cigarette and stood up from the table. "I've a hankering for another elderberry beer. Either of you boys interested?"

"Sorry Bob," Ed gathered his winning acorns and pushed back from the table. "I best be gettin' back 'fore that hawk comes circlin'. But I will take more of that homemade meat stew yous been makin' every week. Can't get enough of it. So good I licked my bowl clean last time, I did."

Bob laughed and went to the kitchen, returning a few moments later with two steaming bowls of the stew, covered tightly with maple-leaf lids to keep them fresh.

"One for the road," he said, handing it to Ed, who grinned.

"And one for you too, friend." He set the bowl down in front of Gregory whose eyes lit up in delight.

"Although I'm not sure you need it." Bob said, turning to Ed with a wink.

Ed guffawed.

Chapter Three

The next day, Gregory stood in his kitchen with a pounding headache. Even though he was drinking his usual two-bean espresso and making pathetic jokes to himself about *how he was so fat his grandmother must've been a rabbit,* he still felt out of sorts. He had indulged in way too many elderberry brews last night, and it was now mid-afternoon. His head had been pounding so much this morning that he wasn't able to get out of bed until well after lunchtime. He was finally getting around to taking the tree-bark coverings off the windows when there was a loud knock at the door.

Funny, he didn't usually get any visitors during acorn gathering time. When he went to open it he found Bob Ross standing there, holding a bowl of his famous stew, looking distraught.

"Have you heard the news?" Bob asked, pushing his way inside. "Ed didn't make it home last night! His wife stayed up for hours waiting for him, and when she woke up in the morning he still wasn't there. No one's seen him!"

Bob began pacing back and forth across the floor.

Gregory was confused. "What? What are you talking about Bob?"

Bob stopped pacing and gave Gregory a worried look. "Ed. He's missing."

Gregory felt a cold chill sweep over him. "What? How can this be? He was with us last night! You don't think... on his way back home... the hawk..."

When Bob didn't answer Gregory knew that was what must've happened. His headache from the earlier morning was gone, now replaced with the sudden urge to throw up.

"I was down at the bakery this morning," Bob said, despair filling his voice. "It's all anyone is talking about. The whole village is in chaos. The Mayor has been working overtime, going to everyone's homes, trying to reassure them. But Gregory," Bob paused, taking a deep breath, "it doesn't look good."

With a groan, Gregory plopped down into a chair, his head in his hands. After a few moments of silence between the mice, Bob cleared his throat. "Listen, here's some more stew if you want it." He set the bowl down on the table. "Ever since I heard the news this morning I've been obsessively cooking. Only way I can get my mind off things, you know?"

Gregory did know. Bob was always a big cook but ever since the hawk started preying on the area he had been making gallons and gallons of the stew. Gregory knew it was a coping mechanism. Some mice talked through troubles, some ignored them completely. Bob cooked.

"Thanks," Gregory said glumly, raising his head. "It

might be just the thing I need to get over this blasted hangover."

Chapter Four

That week, the Wednesday poker night was canceled. The Mayor was extra busy around town installing more tree-bark window coverings for added safety and neither Gregory nor Bob felt up to playing without Ed there. His body had yet to be found but everyone knew without saying it that the hawk would have taken the whole carcass. They ate everything and never left anything behind for the family except a few bloodstains and permanent emotional damage.

The following week, however, Bob decided that the three mice should get together for their usual poker night. "We need to try to get our heads out of this gloomy fog, Gregory," he had finally said one evening. "I can't take it much longer."

So, that Wednesday the trio gathered at Bob's place for a light-handed game. They tried drinking elderberry beer and even upped the stakes to six acorns apiece, but after two failed games and forced conversation it was clear the night was not going to be a success.

The Mayor was the first to admit it, pushing back his chair with a sad frown and folding his paws on his lap. Gregory stared at the acorns on the table not caring if he won or lost for the first time ever. He looked over at Bob.

"Sorry friend. I know you tried. But it's just not the same."

Bob gave a sad smile and nodded.

Chapter Five

The next night as Gregory sat at home wallowing in
the sadness at the loss of his friend and his inability to lose any
weight, his eyes lit upon Bob's bowl of stew, now licked clean,
lying in a heap with the other dirty dishes in the sink. He tried
to tell himself it was kindness, his idea to suddenly return the
bowl to Bob days later than he should have. But the truth was
that he was lonely and couldn't take sitting at home by himself
anymore. Bringing the bowl back to Bob would simply serve as
a means for him to get out of the house, a way to hang out with
a friend who shared his misery.

Quickly, Gregory took a rag and wiped the bowl clean,
then put on his jacket and headed outside with the bowl under
his arm.

At first he was nervous, looking up at the sky for the
circling white underbelly of a hawk. It was the first time he had
been out later than he should have and the streets were empty.
All the houses had tree-bark covering up the light in their
windows.

It was dark and quiet.

When Gregory heard the rustle of grass he began to
pick up his pace. It was probably just a rabbit, but even so,
every sound spooked him until he was running full on down
the street.

Finally, he reached Bob's house. Leaning against the
door and heaving, Gregory once again cursed his chunky frame.
Some easy pickings he'd be! He would never be able to outrun
the other mice, let alone a hawk.

With a suffering groan, Gregory raised his paw and
knocked on Bob's door.

No one answered.

Gregory knocked again, louder. *Maybe Bob is in the*

kitchen cooking and can't hear the door over the rattle of his pots and pans. Gregory thought. After two more knocks with no answer, he slowly turned the doorknob and eased the door open.

It swung on its hinges easily, not even making a creaking sound. Gregory let himself inside and closed the door behind him. The house was bathed in pitch black. Fumbling, he cursed aloud when he smashed into the side of a bookcase instead.

"Bob!" he called desperately. "Where are you? Are you home?"

Finally, after a few insufferable moments Gregory's eyes became more accustomed to the darkness and he could make out a faint light coming from under the kitchen door. Relieved, he shuffled across the room toward the light. When he got to the kitchen door, he called out.

"Finally! Bob, you need to turn some lights on in this place..." and pushed the door open. The words died on his lips.

There against the far wall, leaning over the boiling kettle, were Bob and the Mayor.

Only something about the way they were standing huddled together, laughing, made Gregory pull up short.

At the sound of the door the two mice whirled around and Gregory screamed. There were red blood stains covering their snouts, dripping red puddles gathering on their whiskers, and warm congealed red globs trailing down their coats, splashing in little droplets on the kitchen floor. The smell was horrible. The air felt thick and rank, almost suffocating.

Gregory screamed again.

"What... what..." he stuttered. The Mayor and Bob exchanged amused glances.

"My dear Gregory," the Mayor said, walking closer, backing Gregory against the wall. "It seems you have decided to appear at a rather inopportune moment." Gregory turned his head to the side, squeezing his eyes shut.

The Mayor's face was covered in slick red and his eyes had a maniacal gleam. Slowly, as if in a dream, the Mayor reached out a paw and stroked the side of Gregory's face. Gregory flinched.

"I... I don't understand..." he stuttered. "What are you guys doing? I thought we were all supposed to stay home because of the hawk..."

Bob, still standing over by the boiling kettle, began to laugh. It was a strange laugh, one that screeched and tilted up at the end. Gregory opened his eyes, unable to believe this sound had come out of his good friend.

"My dear, sweet, stupid, fat Gregory," Bob muttered, stirring the kettle. "You never do understand anything, do you? You couldn't even find your own tail if it wasn't attached to your fat behind."

The Mayor grabbed Gregory forcibly by the shoulders and shoved him down into one of the chairs. It was all Gregory could do not to stare at the table where just a few short days ago he had sat laughing, trying to play a game of poker with his two friends. It didn't seem like the same place or even the same memory. What had happened?

The Mayor, as if sensing Gregory's question, sat down in the opposite chair and propped his bloody feet up on the table. Gregory shuddered.

"I am up for re-election in the fall, as you know, Chubby."

Gregory flinched. It was the first time the Mayor had ever used the derogatory word with him and it made his heart beat faster - the way a captured animal's does when cornered, confronted by its predator.

"I love being this town's Mayor, Gregory. I live for it. And not everyone in this village appreciates all my efforts."

Gregory remembered back to all the times he had treated the Mayor disrespectfully, talking bad about him behind his back to Bob and Ed.

"The town is losing faith in me," the Mayor continued, "If I don't win the election I will lose my job. I need this job, Gregory. I am good at it. I'm damn good at it!"

The Mayor leaned forward, his feet dropping to the floor with a loud thud, focusing in a little too intensely on Gregory. His eyes looked strange, like the pupils were two different sizes and it made Gregory's heartbeat climb.

Finally, the Mayor broke his gaze and leaned back in the chair, cleaning his teeth with one of his bloody whiskers. He worked the whisker in and out, in and out, and it made a horrible scratching sound. He continued talking.

"So I invented the hawk story, you see."

Gregory just blinked. The Mayor gave an awful smile.

"Listen Chubby. You obviously are too thick to get it. Doesn't surprise me. I'm sure all you think about is food. So let me break it down for you. I made up the hawk. There never was one. With my plan, there would be a few casualties, the people would get scared, and then I would come in and save the day with my tree-bark window cover idea. People would be ecstatic; I would be a hero, and bam!"

He pounded his bloody paw on the table, sending red globs flying onto Gregory's face, who shuddered and gagged.

"I would be a hero, and the people would re-elect me in gratitude."

Gregory just stared.

"But... but..." he finally managed to squeeze out of his throat, which was tight and scratchy in fear, constricting his speech. "But... Ed... Where's Ed?"

At that moment Bob Ross stepped away from the kettle and plunked down a steaming bowl of stew on the table in front of Gregory. The stew sloshed in the bowl, spilling over the sides.

Bob leaned in, so close that his bloody whiskers brushed the tip of Gregory's nose. He whispered something in an icy voice.

"Gregory. Can you smell what Bob Ross is cooking?"

The End

THE INGENIOUS JUVENESCENT DONNY KEE

Josh Cook

You're a good boy, a Catholic boy, a boy of about ten or fifteen, depending on who asks. Your mother works all day and comes home smelling like lemon and chemicals and Werther's caramels. You have a plan, not only to take over the world, but to make it your hump-backed butler, someone who eats your scraps and has no sense of humor, someone who makes jokes like, "Can you smell what Bob Ross is cooking?" You, the great Donny Kee, will do this. You will champion the world by stealing your neighbor's dog, Spencer Bachus. The gravity of that nomenclature eludes; you heard the plosives pop on CNN, that channel that seems to both boost and diminish your mother's need for the bottles atop the fridge. Bachus: because it sounds dopey, light and airy like a cinnamon bun. Bachus: because every time the commentators holler the name, it sounds like Swedish blood boiling.

Dopey? Yes. Lazy? Affirmative. But, the mutt will do because, in addition to the twelve hours a day it spends moping on the back deck, you need a sidekick.

You've spent all morning warming up to this moment—stomping goombas, hurling fireballs and hurtling piranha plants, conquering surrogate bullies—until, for the last time, your d-d-damn cat spooks and somersaults over the torn couch, flopping onto the grape-juice stain. This freezes your Nintendo training apparatus for the third and last time (And no, you can't even think a swear without it sounding like a stutter). Despite the daylight, you dress in black. You smear your face with your mother's LS-15, Siren Red, and venture outside.

The lilac bushes that separate your house from your neighbors' twirl in the chinook. Helicopter seeds chop like little evildoers. You fashion a shield out of a rusted piece of drainpipe half-buried in the leaves, the leaves that were neither raked last autumn, nor the autumn before that. You squint through the bushes and say, Bachus, Bachus, Bachus, but the dumb mutt just sits there as sad as yesterday.

Yesterday: homeroom: you wore your Magic Johnson jersey with the pseudo-matching shorts your mother brought home from Goodwill. You had said Avery, Avery Johnson, not Magic, was your favorite. She said what's the difference? And would you rather have no jersey at all? Ramón Pinochet, a squirmy little latino ninth-grader with spiked hair and a wheeze, culled you over to the hacky-sack circle and said, Nice flips, pinching his shirt as if to indicate yours. You tried not to laugh, but probably did. Probably snorkeled, like that pea-brained Norwegian concurrence, the inhaling bark that goes *heeeyump, heeeyump*. And they tossed you the hacky-sack, but when you went to kick, Ramón swatted the hacky-sack aside, and with a swift pinch and a tug, sent your shorts a-sailing to the ground. Underwear and all.

Bachus, bachus, you hail through the purple shrubs. You pluck a flower and suck the honey-like sweetness for good luck. You imagine that the lilac flower is actually one girl in the thousand that make up your harem; that the spritz of honey is luck from a goddess, an elixir in a shot glass that will add to your aura of fortitude and disguise your blubbery body. You don't know how long you lean there. When you open your eyes you've dropped your shield, your imagination akimbo with immodest women and various scents of sugar-spritzing. You let your lips loose into a raspberry and shake your head from side to side. You squint through the trees and see your geriatric neighbor, as white a variety as they come, and say, I'm gonna get your pup, Pinocchio. His large nose offends you, even scares you a little, makes you feel like a shovel is being scraped across the pavement of your inner ear. And then: The Twitch. It hits you. A whole-bodied jostle to unfurl The Ugly, each part, wriggling and shaking and flexing and flapping. Some days you Twitch in the bathroom stall after thugs like Pinochet grab your love handles from behind and pretend to water ski. It's been a week since you last Twitched, and you're ashamed, here, amidst your knight-errantry, flouncing like a half-dead koopa.

You hold your breath. You wait for Pinocchio to hobble inside. Cloaked, covered by the bushes, wedged between the forgotten canoe and the balled up tarp, you lower to the ground and retrieve your shield. The rust chafes against your palm. As you turn and step into the bushes, you tighten your grip and hear Bachus whine. You feel a lava-like heat drip down your back. Your temples pulse until your teeth hurt. The wildfire spreads to your hand. But this hot-spell doesn't stop you. It nudges you toward The Noseinator.

The fence, wooden and rickety, at chest-height, offers no slick foothold. Resolution: conjure as many images and memories of days like yesterday. Pinochet's minions, your mother's chemical stink, the jeering tyrants of homeroom, your father's abstruse whereabouts, the fat rolls on your feet, the offensively minuscule portions at school lunches—the list abides you over the fence. In a flourish of ungodly stretching and pulling and tearing, in a breakneck daydream you hear the blast of trumpeters trumpeting, see the gallivanting harem, and feel the soon-to-be preserved pup licking your face.

You lunge once more, somersaulting to the ground, shattering a thousand bones in the name of the father, the son, and the holy ghost. You cross yourself. There is a yapping. Bachus. There are clouds. Angels? Your ears rage a violent fire. The shield broke your fall. Or perhaps it broke your back? You pat yourself all over and realize full feeling, but when you run your hands down your face, you feel something viscous trickle down your cheek. You look at your hand. At first you think it's your mother's number LS-15, but you soon declare laceration. There's a pulse there. You make a fist. You say Game Over in a robot voice.

How many days do stitches have to stay in? What degree of injury constitutes rehabilitation? Will you scream or just whine? How about a good Twitch? Will you slither back inside and hide your hand from your mother until it heals? Your neighbor stands over you and yells indecipherables. As he lurches toward the house and then back toward you dialing a cordless phone, you forget about his nose. From the other end of the phone, you hear your mother shout strings of curses you didn't know existed.

You don't care to strain to listen, because your neighbor, The Artist Formerly Known As The Noseinator, shakes his jowls, covers the earpiece, rolls his eyes, and whispers a hex: Pizza. He hangs up. Sighs. Quite a wind bag, your mom, pardon my German. Your eyes do a dance: Pizza? No, he says. And then follows with two complete sentences. Two words both nouns and verbs and everything in-between, better than a harem and hero combined: Pizza. Rolls.

Good To Know

Nate Watters

I awoke with a buzz in my belly. He was coming today. I sat on the edge of my bunk, petting my stomach and smiling.

This is how it used to be, I used to wake up happy and free. In my best days, the sounds of his feet and his little boy bulldozer noises had been my gentle alarms. After kissing my sleeping wife and rolling from the sheets, I would walk down our creaky steps, rubbing the crust from the edges of my eyes. Usually, he would hear me coming and he would stop his game and run to me. Then we would go about our morning rituals, making coffee, hot chocolate, watching the birds at the feeder, planning the day. Every so often though, I would get lucky, and he would not hear me coming downstairs, he would keep playing. And I would watch him. I loved just watching him.

I had not seen him in eleven years.

There is no family in prison. He is not downstairs playing with the cats or building a cabin out of boxes. There is no coffee to make. They make it for you, it's pitiful, it's cheap, it's watered down shadow-coffee. The food is the same, all of it tastes like a knock-off of the real thing.

I used to make perfect omelets, fluffy and cheesy, with eggs from the neighbor's chickens. Sometimes, my son would come with me to pick up the eggs. He loved to guess which chicken laid which egg. Our neighbor would laugh, and tell him he had no idea which chicken laid which eggs. There were too many. One morning, my son suggested that the farmer tape a different colored marker to each chicken's butt, so it would mark the egg as it came out. Then he would know which egg came from which chicken.

The farmer laughed and said, "Are you sure he's your son? He seems a lot smarter than you."

"His mom, he gets his brains from his mom."

"Mom gave me my brains?"

I laughed, partly at the question and partly at the way his thick hairy caterpillar eyebrows nearly kissed whenever he asked a question.

"Well," I paused. I took his questions seriously. My father had been a joker. I famously told the entire 2nd grade class that my great grandfather had been a gorilla. I had not been joking, I believed my father. I told my class that my great grandfather had been an escaped gorilla from a circus that had been passing through Dublin. My grandfather, who had been half gorilla, became a vaudeville entertainer and magician by the name of The Magnificent Caped Ape. Of course, I wasn't as hairy and strong as him, because I was only 1/8th gorilla.

The laughter of the class didn't hurt, what hurt was figuring out that my Father had lied. I wasn't going to ever lie to my son.

"Mom and Dad gave you a little bit of our selves, then you used those pieces of us and built you. So, Mom didn't give you a brain but you used the little bits we gave you to make a brain. It's like Legos. We gave you those and you built all sorts of cool stuff, right?"

I could tell he wasn't satisfied as we walked. Neither was I. Then he looked up at me, smiling, his eyebrows were back in their place. "Oh, it's like the seeds we used for the garden."

"Yes! That's it. Seeds!" I roughed up his hair. "Wow,

you definitely did get your brains from your Mom."

"What did I get from you?"

"Eyebrows." He tried looking up at his eyebrows as he held my hand and walked back towards home.

"Morning sunshine." My cellmate's deep, morning voice tore me away from my memories, from walking back home along the path, and dropped into reality, my cell. 10 by 15, cinderblocks, no windows.

"Good morning, Senator."

"Hmmm, you're chipper. You finally taking my advice? Guilt is for suckers. You are innocent. We are what we are, human beings."

I was surprised he stopped there, the Senator, surprisingly, loved to talk. Outside, he had talked himself out of a thousand jams, I had heard about them all. But his one thousandth and one jam had been too sticky, he was in for 12 to 16. Same as me. We were good cell mates; he was on the opposite side of the spectrum politically, socially, and spiritually. He loved to stump and preach - it was my version of hell.

Hell is exactly what I wanted. I deserved it. That day, however, I allowed myself some hope of redemption and a crumb of joy.

"No, I am still guilty as hell."

"So, why are you cheery this morning? I mean look at you, you are up early, already dressed, combing your three hairs, and ready to go. What happened? Did you have a dream last night? Huh? Did you dream you had a full head of hair? Were you at a pub singing songs with big bosomed Irish Catholic girls? Were they running their fingers through your hair as they poured beer down your throat?"

"No." I laughed.

"Oh, those girls were in my dreams. Only they weren't stroking my hair, they were stroking,"

"My boy is coming to visit." I didn't want to hear about his dreams today.

The Senator sat up on his bunk, "You don't say." His eyes sparkled. "That's great! Family is number one in my book. That's the problem with this country these days, not enough family time. I'm glad to hear he's coming by." He shook my hand. I had only seen him like this a couple times, it was disarming, nearly hypnotizing. His eyes sparkled, his dimples dimpled. I understood how he had weaseled his way into office and out of trouble so many times.

He continued to talk as we waited for roll call, but I wasn't listening. I was still buzzing. Thinking about home.

He was my only son, but we had planned on having more. We had wanted two more. We wanted to raise the little pack in the country, with trees and creeks and each other as their best friends. And she and I would be best friends and lovers and parents and artists. Then, I broke down. I don't remember much about the whole thing. I remember his face when he found out. He didn't say anything at first. His eyes were painful, I could feel them inside me, screaming, kicking, bashing my heart. Yet he just stood silent and hurt.

He had not been there. He had been at his grandparents. They had to tell him the news, I had no control. I had no idea how they told him or what they told him. I deserved what I got though, I deserved worse. Although, I do not know what could be worse than the scorn of your child.

"Why? Why Daddy? Why?" Over and over, he started crying, blubbering as he sat in a chair across from me. I was in handcuffs in a small room in the local sheriff's office. There was a small card table and a water cooler. A deputy stood by the door. Kindly, they had allowed me to see my son, just him and me, no in-laws or social services, just him and me. I wanted to face him. I wanted him to hate me, to grind me up. I got what I wanted. His grandparents had to carry him away as he kicked and screamed. "WHY DADDY? WHY? WHY?"

"I don't know, I don't know. I don't know."

I truly didn't know then, but I know now. The lawyers and the physiatrist blamed it on a temporary chemical imbalance caused by stress, genetics, and jealousy. I disagree. Sure I was stressed. Sure my father had beaten the shit out of us as kids. Sure, I was not thrilled with the affair. But that's not what broke me, and I did break. It *was* all chemicals, because everything is chemicals. I broke because my fear chemicals took over. I was scared that she was going to leave, that she was going to tear down our cabin, that she was going to stop eating omelets, and that she was going to forget about the other two kids.

That's the reason, but that's not the justification. There is no justification. I will never forgive myself, but maybe he will forgive me. It's the only thing I hope for anymore, and he is coming today. The first time in 11 years, maybe he is ready. Each step I have taken in the last 11 years has been toward this moment, toward his forgiveness.

Lost in my thoughts, I ate the tasteless oatmeal. Maybe today will be the first step back home. I barely heard the voices around me, but Chester, the relentless jerk, kept pushing buttons until I looked up.

"Hey Ginger, I heard your kid's visiting today. Is he a redhead, too? He got anger problems like his old man? You sure you want to let him get close? He might whoop your ass"

I just smiled and kept chewing. I was on cloud nine. My son had never been angry. When he was young I had to teach him how to be angry. After watching yet another child take his toy and push him over, with no reaction from him, but a quivering of the lips and a crunching of the eyebrows. I decided to teach him how to get mad. I told him to yell, get angry, stomp his foot, push back, and stand his ground. I showed him how to do it. He only fell down and burst into tears.

Unfortunately, another parent at the park had thought I was yelling at him and stomping my foot and pushing my child. Protective services was called, and a headache ensued.

My oatmeal was finished, my coffee nearly done. I smiled to myself as I remembered dealing with the well-intentioned, overworked social worker.

"What are you smiling about?" As I had daydreamed, my only real friend had sat down across from me.

"Oh hey Reverend. How's it going? Today is the big day, my son is visiting"

"That's right, I had forgotten. That's wonderful, you must be excited. It's been a while. You gonna tell him what you want tell him?"

"I don't know. We will see. I want to hear what he has to say first." I said and I looked at the clock. "I better get going. He's coming at ten. I better get to my cell. See ya Rev."

The reverend smiled one of his benevolent smiles and said, "God Bless. I'll be praying for you."

"I bet he is a good dad," I thought as I moved toward the door.

I was only in the cell a half hour before they came to get me. I had never been more nervous in my life, I needed my son back. I would never get her back, I knew that, but I still hoped for him. I floated down the halls, I was a balloon tied to the guard's wrist. I ducked my head as we walked through the door and searched the room.

He was sitting alone in a corner table, opposite from the play area and the snack machines. I almost stopped and ran back to my cell. I suddenly wanted to be locked down and under covers. What if he was here to say goodbye? What if he was here to tell me he hated me and he never wanted to see me again? If I stayed in my cell, I could at least have a hope. I was sticking my hope's neck out to be chopped.

"I am being overdramatic." I thought, like my Italian mother. I had not thought of her in ages. I felt too ashamed, but as I walked toward my son, I thought of my mother. Waving her spoon at me as I dipped my finger in the cake batter. She would wave her spoon so menacingly, but behind the spoon, I could see her thin lips smiling. For some reason, I have never missed my mother as much as I missed her then, walking across the visiting room.

I went to hug my son. He did not stand up, it was an awkward hug. I wanted to embrace him, bear hug for hours. Instead, he lifted his left hand up, patted my shoulder, and let go. So I did, too. I sat down.

"Thank you so much for coming." I know I had tears in my eyes.

"Yeah." He nodded. He was wearing a t-shirt, silkscreened with a picture of Bob Ross wearing a chef's hat and holding his palate and brush in his left hand. In a bubble, it said "Can you smell what Bob Ross is cooking?"

"Nice shirt." I laughed.

He looked down at it, as if he forgot what he was wearing. "Oh, yeah, it's one of Mom's new ones. She has been selling em like crazy."

"Has she? Great! T-shirts, huh? Is she making dresses and the shawls anymore?" It hurt to talk about her, my stomach clinched tightly around itself.

"It still hurts her to smile." He looked at me. I had hoped to catch up before we took off the bandages.

"Me too."

"What? You too? Nobody bashed your face in with a vase." He was a teenager, full of anger and chemicals. He breathed heavily as he stared me down. It was then I noticed that, except for his eyebrows, he had inherited his mother's Russian good looks. High cheek bones, grey blue eyes, dirty blond hair left to grow long and covering his eyebrows. He was taller too, taller than I imagined him. I could tell that even though he was sitting down.

"You're right." I whispered.

"I know." He looked away and he pulled keys from his pocket. "I don't know why I came. I should,"

"You drove here? You have your license?" Of course, he was almost 17, I had nearly forgotten. In all my letters I had never asked. I had never been a big fan of cars. I barely knew the difference between a sedan and a coupe. "What are you driving?"

My son studied my face, "I'm only here because my therapist thinks it's a good idea, so does Mom by the way. I am not so sure. I don't need another Dad. I was six when you left, Carl has been around for 8 years, he is two years more my Dad than you are. And he has never tried to kill Mom." He stopped and let it sink in

"I guess I'm here to find closure. That's what they called it."

I stared at him, and I realized the truth. He was here to cut me away. I should have been devastated, but I was not. All this time, I had kept myself afloat by convincing myself that I had reason to hope. I convinced myself that I needed that hope. Then, there, I suddenly saw that hope vanish. In order to survive, I had tricked myself into believing he was still my son, that he was still 5 years old and looking up at me. But he was not that little boy anymore, he wasn't here to forgive me. He was there to forget me, to cut me from his life. Suddenly, I was lost, floating free. I had nothing tethering me to this earth. My son's face grew smaller and smaller as I drifted up, up and away. I was terrified, I struggled to breathe, and somehow it felt right, as if this is what I wanted the whole time.

It was time for me to go.

"I'm sorry. I am sorry." I repeated. As if repetition would convince him to forgive me, but guilt and apologies was all I had to offer. He placed his keys on the table and took a deep breath, when he exhaled it blew his bangs from his forehead. He looked around the room. He was tapping his foot nervously as he sat there. He must have got that from me, too. Eyebrows and nervous ticks. Nightmares and issues. These are what I passed to my son. It was time for this ghost to move on and stop haunting the living. I stood up.

"Thank you for coming. I loved, love, you. Goodbye." My words were rough-cut and heartless, I was still drifting, feeling myself slipping away. It was over just like that, less than ten minutes. I needed to leave. I turned to go. I walked toward the door.

"Hey! Before you go, I want to know why. Why did you do it?" His eyebrows dipped below his bangs. He was standing now.

A thousand excuses whistled through my head, but I decided on the truth.

"I was afraid of losing you." I waved and smiled. I thought about giving him a hug, but I decided to just walk away.

A CAUTIONARY TALE

Christopher Tradowsky

for Sean Owens

Faust was multitasking. He was eating lunch in front of the television, watching his favorite cooking show, and daydreaming of a better life. The hostess was plucking blue hydrangeas from her garden in the Hamptons. In his head he flitted between questions imponderable and fully ponderable: Who will care for him when he's toothless, and why is Sriracha hot sauce so, so delicious? How had he come to this point in life? And who first thought it was a good idea to drink toasted bean-water? Are there any slums in the Hamptons? If so, could he afford a carriage house there? Or a tree house, or even a dog house, in that slum?

All at once there was a swift snapping like that of a spark plug, a strobe flash, a trail of smoke and a stench of molten metal, as if someone had just fired up an arc-welder in the nearby recliner. Faust turned from the flash, but when he looked again at what had been an empty chair, there sat a middle-aged woman, slender and spotlessly dressed in a gray wool suit, like a secretary from a Frank Capra film. She had a militaristic posture and a hawkish face that seemed to have been afflicted with a mild case of late-stage cubism. Faust was so startled that he gripped his shawarma desperately with both hands, until it unloaded its contents down his front and into his lap.

The woman spoke: "You are surprised to see me. And yet you summoned me."

"I beg your pardon?" Faust said, wiping hummus and lamb shrapnel from his lap.

"I never come unless someone has summoned me," she offered, as if that explained everything. She had a thick German accent.

"Excuse me," Faust said, genuinely confused, "But aren't you Ute Lemper?"

The woman laughed tersely, and said "No, no. *Naturlich,* I am the devil."

"In the shape of Ute Lemper?"

The woman sighed. "Where is your sense of history? I am Eva Braun."

"Oh, I see. You're the devil..."

The woman nodded.

"And you're meant to be Eva Braun..."

"I *am* Eva Braun..."

"Yeah—but your face—I think you got something about the face wrong."

Eva waved a schoolmarm's finger at Faust. "You are certain you want to argue with me? I lose very few arguments."

"Okay, so, Eva Braun, alright, but why not Hitler?" Faust offered, "just out of curiosity?"

"Oh well," Eva rolled her eyes, "That would be kind of obvious, wouldn't it? A bit expected?"

"I suppose, but at least I would be certain who I'm dealing with. You'd make your entrance and one could say, with all certainty, 'now there's the personification of evil,' rather than thinking, oh, hey—it's that screechy German cabaret singer from the 90's that nobody likes."

Eva huffed a bit. With a little flourish of her left hand

she pulled a lit cigarette out of mid-air and began to suck smoke through an ivory holder. Faust moued disapprovingly, but she seemed not to notice. "I'm just saying," Faust went on, "just on the level of brand recognition, you might have done better with Anne Coulter, or Dick Cheney?"

"Dick Cheney is still alive," Eva said.

"Yes, thanks to you..."

Eva French inhaled. "Look, we can quibble about avatars, or we can get down to the business of what I can do for you. My time is precious, I am very in demand these days..."

"That's fine," said Faust, "you may see yourself out, since I certainly did not summon you."

"You did indeed, just this moment. You see, I respond directly to a surplus of human need. Whenever a mortal is so immersed in their own desire..."

"I'm going to stop you right there," said Faust. "Would you please not smoke in my apartment? I mean, I'm sure *you're* not concerned about lung cancer or tracheotomies..."

"*Ach, verdammt*" Eva took a long drag, and after searching the coffee table in vain for an ashtray, dropped the cigarette into a can of Mr Pibb. Smoke swarmed from her mouth as she cursed. "You Germans are such tight-asses."

"You *are* purporting to be *Eva Braun*, aren't you?"

"I fear you are not grasping the situation. I am not *actually* Eva Braun, I am actually the *Prince of Darkness.*"

"Yes, but you see," said Faust, "There's where I'm unsure. I'm still not convinced that you're more than a washed-up cabaret act with a few cute parlor tricks up her sleeve..."

If this was an affront, Eva seemed unperturbed, and continued with a well-rehearsed pitch, like any good saleswoman. "As I say, I respond directly to human need. And so it is: when a mortal is so immersed in their own desire that they spontaneously wish for three things at once, in their very soul, then I will always appear."

"Okay, well then," Faust replied with relief, "you seem to have gotten your wires crossed, because I was simply sitting here, enjoying my lunch, which incidentally you have ruined, thank you very much, and I was not wishing for anything at all, let alone three things at once. In my very soul."

"Is that so?" Eva smiled beatifically, "You didn't even wish for your favorite Sriracha hot-sauce for your shawarma?

"No, no, absolutely not!" Faust insisted.

This was a lie. He had, in fact, just run out of his beloved Sriracha. He longed for it intensely while he tucked into his rather bland sandwich. And though Faust hated lying, somehow he felt he could still hold moral high ground over someone who willingly claimed to be the girlfriend of Hitler.

"Alright then," said the stylish secretary of evil, "But you are watching one of your favorite cooking shows, *nicht war?* Like you watch every day? And weren't you just wishing, as you so often do, that you could smell those fabulous lobster tails, sautéing there in all that clarified butter?"

Faust could do nothing but blink in astonishment. For she was right, he had just been longing, desperately it would be fair to say, to inhale the inimitable scent of sautéing lobster. Just as he realized this, the television screen seemed to disgorge itself of an irresistible cloud of succulent fumes: of butter, and shellfish, and fennel, and a broth rich with aromatics. Faust closed his eyes and succumbed. "That's right," Eva said, "close your eyes and breathe deep, breathe it all in! Is it not delectable? Can you smell what Bob Ross is cooking for you?"

With that, Faust's eyes sprung open. "Bob Ross? Bob Ross? That's Ina Garten you Teutonic twit! How could you possibly mistake Ina Garten for Bob Ross? Ina Garten is the reigning queen of the Food Network. Bob Ross is that PBS painter who died, like, 15 years ago!"

"Now, how should I know that?" protested Eva, "I've been dead since 1945."

"I thought you said you *weren't* Eva Braun; that you are actually the *Prince of Darkness?*"

"Oh, sometimes I absorb the limitations of my avatars."

"No kidding? Yes, come to think of it, I had heard that Eva Braun was a half-wit. Look, I would not mess with Ina Garten! She would be *furious* if she knew you had mistaken her for Bob Ross. And she used to work for the government—the CIA I think. She's probably had people rubbed out for lesser offenses!"

"Is that so?" Eva looked very smug. "Well Herr Faustus, if you think you're so clever, it was actually *Julia Child* who worked for the CIA. And I am very aware of every time *she* had someone rubbed out."

"Who the hell are you?" Faust cried, exasperated, "and why are you ruining my afternoon?"

"Oh, tsk, Faustus, don't lose your temper, when I have so much to offer you! I was just about to answer your third wish, your fondest wish. It is within my power to realize your most intoxicating dream."

"I'm drawing a blank here," said Faust, "does it have anything to do with hot sauce? Or the Food Network's weekend programming?"

"No, you doof." Eva leaned toward him and said in a sulfurous stage whisper, as if her rotten lisp would make the offer more enticing, "The hareem, the hareem..."

"The wha? The harem? I never wished for a harem!"

"Don't be an imbecile, all men wish for a hareem. Every red-blooded man since Sardanapalus has wished for a hareem. They wish it when awake, they wish it when asleep. It is one of the few universals: men dream of hareems."

"Okay, number one: stop saying hareem. Number two:

you really need to start working on your background research. Bob Ross was not a chef. And I am about as gay as a marabou stork..."

"You know those things are carrion eaters," Eva interjected, "They are just fluffy-bellied vultures..."

"...Further proving my point, which is, I'm so gay that everywhere I walk I am accompanied by jazz flute. The last thing I would wish for is a harem! I'd be infinitely more likely to wish for *harem pants,* or to wish that I could pull them off... you know, I'm not a young slip-of-a-thing anymore, and silk organza is so unforgiving to the figure..."

At this point Eva stood up, and began to pace. "Faust, you are incorrigible. So you want a hareem filled with men! Nubile, sinewy-smooth ones? Or broad, hairy lumberjacks? A selection? A flight of sodomites, slinging martinis? You name it, I can provide!"

"Ugh, no thank you! The whole thing sounds filthy! Where on earth would I keep them all? And just the laundry costs alone are boggling—I'd have to get a service—and who would feed all those bears and cubs? I mean, on my salary? Honestly, I don't think you've really thought this through. Not to mention: deeply un-hygienic!

"Oh, you Germans are so prissy!"

"That's another thing. Do your homework! Whoever you are, Prince of *dumkopfs*—your royal—loathsomeness—I'm not even German, I'm Mexican. My name is Manuelo Faust. Perhaps you got the wrong apartment in the first place?"

"Look," said Eva, still pacing and obviously disturbed, "I thought you had summoned me. My mistake. I'm sure it was me. Even so, you are the most annoying creature I have ever met, living or dead, human or demon, and just keep in mind I'm saying this *as the devil.* In my line of work you meet *a lot* of irritating people. How about we forget the whole thing happened? And you could do me a big favor by simply never wishing for anything ever again."

With that, Eva Braun spread her arms wide and operatically, like a temp-agency Nosferatu. Faust thought the effect would have been much more impressive with a cape. Then she winked out of sight, rudely, without so much as an *aufwiedersehen.*

"Drama queen," said Manuelo Faust, as he went to the kitchen for a dish-cloth.

A wicked, molten smell lingered. On the television Ina Garten was demonstrating, for what seemed like the bazillionth time, how to make her "outrageous brownies!"

Hotdish Hell

Randy Holland

When I die, I'm going to the Land of 10,000 Burning Lakes. Or Hotdish Hell, as I like to call it. The pious just call it Hell though, with lakes of fire scalding sinners like me.

Hell is my destination for being a cheating son of a bitch in the annual hotdish competition held in our town's Lutheran church basement. When I win, I'll get my public access cooking show picked up by a major cable network. My culinary arts degree will finally pay off. But first I have to beat the five-time winner, Bob Ross. Bob Ross, now with his own TV show on PBS called Hotdish Heaven. Bob Ross, the chef who can turn beef and beets into fine cuisine with nothing but cream of mushroom soup and his secret ingredient.

The church's basement is humid from all the cooking. Extension cords run everywhere to power the hot plates crucial to every cook. Nothing is reheated in this contest. You have to cook everything from scratch within a four-hour time frame. Some chefs need all four hours. I need two. Bob needs all four, but mainly to sign his bestselling cookbook.

Everyone asks, "Can you smell what Bob Ross is cooking?" Everyone tries to detect Bob's secret ingredient. Everyone fails.

The church ladies say their secret ingredient is love, which is true. The only thing Lutheran ladies lie about is that all Scandinavian countries are equal. But some of these ladies are actually using one of Bob's secret ingredients by accident. Just not enough to win.

I know this because I've figured out Bob's secret. A secret even he doesn't fully understand. The bastard is winning with umami. What's umami? A Japanese scientist was the first to figure out that our tongues detect more than sweet, sour, bitter, and salty tastes. Umami is the fifth taste, although you don't really taste it. It enhances other tastes. And it's in mushrooms—big time. Get it? Cream of mushroom soup is in lots of hot dishes. By coincidence, Bob just happens to use tons of mushrooms. But too much umami backfires. That's why Bob's going down. I'm slipping an overdose of umami into his crock pot.

I just need a distraction. Bob's ego is his weakness, so I stride over with a copy of his cookbook. "My mother would love if you autographed her copy of your book."

As I hold the cookbook over Bob's bubbling hotdish, my hand underneath the book conceals a small vial of umami. I dump in the vial's malicious powder like a professional saboteur, and then hide the vial in my palm. I'm good with card tricks, so my sabotage is done in an instant with Bob suspecting nothing.

Bob smiles and writes in the book, "You should be proud of your son's public-access cable show. Happy hotdishes!" He laughs and says, "Maybe this is your year to win?"

"Maybe," I say. What a gloating asshole. I take the cookbook and excuse myself to tend to my own hotdish.

I taste my entry with ten minutes left until judging starts. It's perfect. I turn the hotplate dial down to low. Faint whiffs of steam rise from crispy tator tots that glisten on top of a bed of wild rice, mushrooms, chicken, and the perfect amount of added umami. I discretely spy on Bob with side-glances.

Within minutes, panic creeps onto Bob's face. He tastes, he stirs. He adds more ingredients, then stirs faster. He tastes again. More panic, more stirring. With only minutes left, his face spasms with confusion.

A buzzer sounds. Time's up. Bob hides his anxiety by flashing his TV smile and bleached teeth. Three judges start tasting clumps from each hotdish. They methodically stop at each cooking station. No words are exchanged, except with Bob. My teeth grind.

My pulse whooshes through my ears, drowning out the church ladies gossiping around me. I know my hotdish sabotage won't be enough to win because Bob's real secret ingredient has nothing to do with the science of taste buds. Don't get me wrong, Bob's hotdishes are good, but they're not worth tweeting about.

The judges strut around: the mayor, the local senator, and the church's pastor. All three are corrupt, although not as corrupt as former Alaskan Senator Ted Stevens, Mister Bridge to Nowhere. They're corrupt because bribery is Bob's key to winning. He sends the judges crates of lefse and lutefisk every Christmas, plus free tickets to his TV show. How do you compete with that?

With a zoom lens and blackmail.

Sure, blackmail is cheating too, but it's for a noble cause. Kind of like gunpowder, which kills people, but funds the Nobel Peace Prize and makes fireworks. Who doesn't love fireworks? So, blackmail can be used for a noble cause, like eliminating the biggest cheater in hotdish history.

Blackmailing the mayor was easy. He and I are fishing buddies, and conversations in ice fishing houses are almost like Holy Absolution. Plus, I know the red-light ice-fishing house is his favorite place to visit, if you know what I mean. His wife finds his warts repulsive, but won't divorce him since she likes all the free coffee she gets as a politician's wife. He won't divorce her since he thinks he'd lose custody of their black lab, which I'll admit is a great dog. So, they have an open marriage, with occasional swinger parties at some remote RV park up north where nobody knows who anybody is. They're both happy, as long as the voting public doesn't find out.

But friend or not, bribery is wrong. So I sent the mayor photos of him getting into and out of the red light fish house with a half-clothed lady I won't name, but all the locals know her specialty. Included with the photos was an anonymous note, "Time to share the glory: Bob Ross's hotdish can never win again, or else." I know my hotdish tastes the best, so there was no need to tell the judges who to vote for. That'd make me a suspect anyway, and I'd hate to be caught and become the butt of a bad Sven and Ole joke.

To blackmail the senator, I sent the same note, but the photos were of his high school daughter doing a Monica Lewinski impression with her class president. I used Photoshop though, it didn't really happen. The senator was squeaky clean until his daughter got a parking ticket last winter. With the new gerrymandered districts his reelection isn't certain, so he'll want to keep her photos out of the headlines and porn sites. I wouldn't really send them anywhere, but he doesn't know that.

Two sex scandals, two judges taken care of.

Blackmailing the pastor was hardest. No lie seemed good enough, so I finally settled on just sending him a vague note that said, "I know what happened at the church's summer camp, and everyone else will too if Bob Ross's hotdish ever wins again." It's a safe bet some scandal happened at the church's summer camp. All summer camps have secrets. But if this blackmail doesn't work, I still have two of the three judges voting against Bob's hotdish. That's enough. Even if just one judge gives Bob a really low score, I'll win. Then there'll be justice.

All three judges finish their taste testing. Bob's fidgeting. I fight back a grin as the judges count down the top ten finishers. Bob finishes seventh. His TV smile vanishes. The humiliation will kill his TV ratings. PBS will need a new hotdish show: my show, from the same self-proclaimed hotdish capital of the world. (Of note, the city council considered calling our town the buckthorn capital of the world, but luckily they picked hotdish capital instead. Don't miss our hotdish parade in the fall, it's a hoot.)

My name's called out. Second place. I'm stunned. The only thing more impressive than winning five times in a row is being the person who defeats a five-time winner. Now that honor has been taken from me. My hopes crumble like dried up lefse.

No network TV show.

No Sons of Norway District Presidency.

No embossed letter from the King and Queen of Norway.

Despite ending Bob's hotdish reign, my justice is denied. I barely hear the winner's name called out. Everyone's stunned. A teenage Swedish bikini team runner-up beat me with green beans, gray mush, and a fried onion topping? That's it? Something smells fishier than lutefisk.

I'm not alone with my conspiracy thinking. The church ladies all have looks that could blister that blonde bimbo's perfect tan. Miss Sweden twirls around in her traditional Swedish folk dress, her yellow skirt fluttering. She winks at the three judges. The mayor and senator smirk. The pastor blushes.

She blathers into a microphone about this being her first year competing, and giggles at how much trouble she had opening the canned soup and green beans. I sit down as she whines about how hard it is to find gluten free ingredients. My guts twist as I imagine her twirling skirts on her new public access TV show, and then syndication on PBS, and then her leaving PBS for the Food Network, and some silly cookbook series she'll write, and her blogging about gluten free hotdishes.

But the worst part of my loss is the whispers and people's pity. I'm a six-time runner-up.

If I'm going to be a scorched swimmer in Hotdish Hell anyway, there's no reason to hold back now. This hotdish hottie will soon be the Food Network's newest celebrity chef—unless there's an accident. A bad accident, so the runner up has to fulfill the hotdish champion's duties. In fact, I think there'll be four bad accidents, including the judges. It's time for a revolution in the hotdish capital. Then this competition will just be about the best chef winning. That'll be me of course, with my secret umami recipe. Then, food science will win, not corruption. Science is worth going to Hell for.

LE GIBBON KING
OF SCOTLAND

Madtheau Wollis

I'm a Wallace.

Entirely by accident as my father told me, as his grandfather told him, and presumably told on down the line until we find ourselves at the Braveheart himself. Apparently, as it goes, everything is an accident in Scotland because as my dear Uncle William put it, "why in all of the seven, blooming hells would you want to be a Scot? We've got the grippe in our bones, the heather tangled in our arses, and the natural inclination to arch our eyebrows evilly towards the oxen heads of this world's ill-bred men."

I've never quite followed what he meant by that.

Uncle William Wallace is the unshorn sheep of the family. He stayed in Stirling, our familial home, as an elected member of the community council when grandfather crossed the Atlantic with his wife and my father. There he has remained since. He is still part of the council but most of his time is spent in the pursuit of tourists' cash and daughters. He often does this dressed as Robin of Locksley, though he tells people he is William Wallace. Mostly because he is William Wallace, that's his name, there's no way around that. Uncle is a character through and through.

In January of 2007, I had the chance to fly out and

stay with my uncle. I had dreamed of going to Scotland since
I was five; dreams involving vivid fields of purple heather, of
shaggy cows, and of odd faery magic. These dreams had created
a life-long fantasy of becoming Scottish, some sort of instant
transformation filled with bright effects, hazy LSD lights,
and wizardry. As I am told, I am also a character through and
through, but mostly of a different sort. The point is that I had
an obsession and that I finally had the financial means to travel
to Scotland with the intent of becoming Scottish myself.

My stay was for a week. Good Uncle William, who
always went by Uncle Illia because he always says he is in
between things and that a proper name should reflect perfectly
upon oneself. He led me across the breach of reality and fantasy
and in doing so has embarrassed me thoroughly to this day. I'll
never set foot in Scotland again.

Here's how it went:

"There's the baby all washed and waxed," Uncle Illia,
arms raised, met me in the town center garbed in a fake beard,
full kilt, cardboard broadsword, and a two-pence grin, "I've
been waiting for an adventure all year!"

"It's January 10th, Uncle."

"Aye, it is. It is, it is, it is. Been long enough hasn't it? It
has. Quick, we're off to the house, the pub, the jail, and then
to breakfast," Uncle bellowed as he grabbed my bag and walked
briskly down the street. Along the way he pointed to several
buildings and houses; even grunted at a few, "'ats what 'at is,
alright," he'd mutter, then smile at several people he knew and
when they passed he'd turn and give them a two-second stare,
eyebrow arched, eyes egged. His one arm swung at his side in a
particular and exaggerated manner, keeping time and balance
as his feet crisscrossed the lines in the cobblestones. Yes, Uncle
Illia, is a tall man, a wide man, and a smelly man. It's best to
walk adjacent to him to spare most, if not all, of your senses.

"You see over there, huh?" Uncle muttered, "You see that house, prim and prime, with the ugly 'goyles hanging their dumb, mean mugs over the roof's edge? That's my folks' old house. A couple from Edinburgh has moved there now. They're historians, they say. They want to be next to the 'Old Saxon culture and ley lines'. Bah! I said, but that's not the matter though now is it? Awfully nice place. Loved living there. Loved it indeed."

As we walked by, a middle aged woman stared out the window at us. When my Uncle looked away, she gave him the two-bird salute and the next few words, though muffled by the glass, were very apparent in their ill intent.
We made it to my uncle's house and the lawn was covered in plastic pink flamingos. Near the window a gnome was placed on top of a stone pier dictating to his minions below.

"Aye there, Finkle," Uncle grinned at the gnome as he opened the door, "keep them birds right in their place for me," he sputtered before tripping over his own doorstep and into his house.

"Damn, the blooming birds! Damn them to hell with its brimstone and Scottish food! Finkle's turned into Einhorn, has he! Setting up the traps has he! Bloody, squatish gnome!"

My bags flew out of his hands, across the doorway, skidded along the floor into the kitchen and remained there for the rest of the night because as soon as my Uncle was up, and his toe was properly cursed for its stupidity, he shut the door, grabbed me by the shoulder and said, "We're off to go break this place, aren't we there, nephew. Let's find the tarnish in old Stirling!"

As we walked, Uncle continued his angry discourse, "Now, nephew, never trust a gnome as far as you can go. Sure they're fine for menial tasks, like making sure that no faery folk steal my birds. You see, they think they're pretty. And they are!

But they're mine! You hear me? That lip wasn't under the door before. Nope. It sees I have a guest and there you go, you saw, it dropped me straight onto my arse."

We wandered the streets for awhile until my Uncle found the pub he was looking for. We ended up at Nicky-Tams on 29 Baker Street. It was a nice enough old place ~ a long wooden bar, white walls with mundane paintings, and a small fire to keep warm in the January weather.
Up on the hill, the castle Stirling was settled in for the night with a cozy blanket of fog. Massive stone walls and sodium lamps helped its eerie persona as it was slowly eaten by the clouds come to Earth.

My uncle sat me down and ordered us both a Barclay Perkins IPA with a side of Bruichladdich. "Up and at'em," he mumbled quickly as we toasted. The pints drained down warm, the whisky warmer, and the bones started their kilning ovens. We did this for awhile; a long while. I filled my Uncle in on my life. He laughed for 4 minutes straight when I told him about my girlfriend's recent religious conversion to Scientology. Then he stood up, told everyone in the bar for a quick round of laughs and sat back down red in the face and sweaty in the palms.

"A bullet's been dodged there. I'd take me a faery folk over one of those nutters. You shouldn't be complaining, I say; a drink a drink a drink, yessir, lets has us another drink."

Just after the fog swallowed the last ray of sunlight, a group of tourists walked into the pub and sat down while removing their scarves and hats. Gold coins started dancing in my Uncles eyes and he mumbled, "here we go laddy. Here. We. Go!"

The group consisted of several people in their late 20's. They were guys and girls who were traveling around Scotland while on break from grad school in Edinburgh. To my memory there were two Germans, a French girl, and two Australians. All of them bug-eyed at the fake-bearded man waving a cardboard broadsword over his head, one- handed, while downing the pint with his other. "Ach! Ach! Ach! I'll give you the fear of Gibson, I will, and the freedom too, as Mad Max would tell ya!" Uncle roared.

Taken aback, the French girl uttered, "*Vieillard, calme toi.*"

Enough was enough, I got up and raced over to try to save them from their papercut beheadings and to try and impress the French girl with my ungainly stupidity. Pint in hand, I stumbled twice, found my step and was over right quick.

"Don' worry, don't worry! He's supposin' to be Mel Gibbons from Bravefart! It's safe, sword not real, and I'm American, so trust me! You remember Bravefart? I know you do," I slurred at the French girl while narrowing my eyes at her, 'You can kill the wimmins but you'll NEVER. GRAB. MY. FREEEDOM!'"

Taking my Uncle's cardboard broadsword and raising it above my head, dropping my pint, and grabbing my own, short sword with the other hand, I stuck the pose. Maybe an 8.5 out of 10. The Russian judge never scores Americans high, anyway.

My Uncle's eyes glowed with pride.

"Nephew... my Nephew everyone!" He proclaimed as he grabbed my hand which was still pointing the sword towards the ceiling, and took a deep bow while the tourists laughed at us; it was the old, fat man and the young, dumb man pissed and plastered for the good of the show. We joined them at their table after that. I grabbed a stool from where I was sitting and pulled it right up to the French girl who had round, alien eyes that shimmered with lively, silverfish hue.

"Have you all seen it, then?" My Uncle asked to our

confusion. "The statue of Mel Gibbons! They ponced him up straight outta Braveheart, they did. Looks like a righteous arse."

"You're lying, and it's Gibson, and he's not a monkey," one of the Aussies spouted off before laughing at the hurt look on my Uncle's face.

"Oh that's for you to decide, now is it? Damn straight he's monkey. And me? Lying! You've a cold heart, Aussie. And to think, your land birthed our savior! The native Gibbons of Australia saved the noble savage of Scotland!"

"It's Gibson," spat out one of the Germans.

Ignoring him, my Uncle growled, "They should ban the contemptible thing. Slap it in chains and let England quarter and staff it, then feed the miserable stones to all the miserable fish in all of miserable England!"

The Aussies chortled and laughed and no one believed Uncle Illia. It seemed too ridiculous that someone would sculpt William Wallace in the image of Mel Gibson. Gibson's like 4 feet tall, Wallace was a giant of a man. But then again, who would know any of this?

The Germans didn't seem too impressed, but the Aussies and the French girl were alright with us. Everyone bought some whisky and drained it while playing a word game involving intricate sexual terminology with an adolescent mindset. My Uncle won.

Eventually we headed out of Nicky Tams and wandered our way to the Albion Scullery with the French girl and Australians in tow.

Stumbling through the door, Uncle was bellowing, "you gave the skirts to the girls and have gone and made everything harder for yourself," as several Englishman walked out. Uncle showed them his 'highland thunder' to their yelling of "poxy, fucking Saxon poof," to Mademoiselle France's, "*Chiens qui reniflent le cul!*" and then suddenly, we were inside, confused

and in a state of glorious upheaval. Drinks were ordered,
my arm was around the French girl, my Uncle's arms were
around both of the Australians and "Gibbons, Mel Gibbons,
the Australian warrior prince of Scottish freedom," was being
toasted.

At some point the Australians lost their wallets and my
Uncle paid for them with his own money. Seemed like a kind
gesture at the moment.

It looked to me as though the French girl's eyes began
to glow as my Uncle began talking of the faery folk that lived in
the Scottish lands. "They're devious folk with devious errands,
they are. If you're thinking that God or the Holy Beast'll put
a stop to them then you've got yourself a bad hand of cards.
They're much older than those quaint folks aren't they now!"
He grinned a toothy grin and looked at me. "You'll bear to find
out someday or somehow, nephew."

I was enraptured. Mostly by booze but it was followed
up with a hearty dose of the imaginary possibility of magic.

I stopped paying attention to Uncle and put most of
it in the French girl whose eyes were mesmerizing and whose
laugh was a little unnerving.

"*Plus, donnez moi plus!*" she raved as she threw down
money on the table for more drinks. The Australians, who held
their own, began necking in the far side of the booth.

"Well look at that, wouldn't ya," Uncle leaning in
for a closer look while raising his glass in a toast, "two and to
youngins with hair on their chins, going at it in the Highlands!"
He leaned back looking impressed. "There's a picture Bob
Ross'd get a good price for. Have you heard of Bob Ross,
nephew? He wastes his time painting amazing landscapes. He's
all over the internet; a better looking Richard Simmons. Anway,
he'd paint that and he could sell it to those English bastards
who walked out earlier, yelling about poxys and poofs as if the

English weren't the biggest fans of bangers in the morning."

I laughed because I didn't know what a banger in the morning was, but I knew what it sounded like. Immaturity becomes me.

"*D'accord. Ça suffit. Tu es ivre et c'est l'heure à partir,*" whispered Mlle France into my ear.

I turned and stared into the silver eyes where I could see waves splashing as if through a telescope. She pushed me out of the booth and we stumbled from the Scullery with my Uncle behind us, singing old Scottish gibberish. She had started speaking French as the drinks progressed.

"I know what you are," I said. "You're of the faery folk. I know what's happening! My Uncle summoned you to help me become a highland shaman!"

The drunken mysticism had struck me as I turned to look at her. The moon had found a way out of the clouds and in the distance a pair of tree limbs aligned perfectly behind her head to look like a small pair of antlers.

"Uncle, look!, 'imma goin to be one of the old folk, like you!"

My Uncle turned slowly, "who you calling old, nephew?"

"*Regarde-toi, minet. Tu trebuches sur les pieds maintenant. Je pense que tu me poursuis, mais nous avons un petit voyage à promener devant nous,*" and with that, Mlle. France imperiously danced ahead.

"Are you speaking the faery language? What language are you speaking? Will I learn it, too?"

Mlle. France turned suddenly and looked at me with her strange eyes, "*Pourquoi tu continues à m'appeler une tapette, tu garçon saoul toi?*"

Yes, I know. I'm dumb. I forgot she was French.

My Uncle caught onto the word faery and had taken it

as a motif. He began to search around him to find any, walking in zigzags up and down the country road we'd found ourselves on.

"Faery, faery, faaaaaaaaaaaaaeeeeeeeeeeerrrrrrrryy," my Uncle screamed and hollered as his fake beard sat around his throat. He was waving his cardboard broadsword over his head, taking strikes at the air when we came upon the statue of William Wallace and all if it's Mel Gibson glory. All four feet of him lording over the land he'd pretended to lose.

"*Mon dieu, il avait raison! C'est Mel Gibson!*"

"C'omm'on erre, nephew," slurred Uncle, "Me and Frenchie have a special mission for you. You're going to climb up that statue, climb right onto the Monkey himself, and you'll spank that Gibbon until it screams 'Freedom!'"

Cackling, my Uncle danced away and procured a camera from the French girl who was chanting, "Fais-le, fais-le!"

"Is this my path to the other worlds? Iz thisz how I become a true Scotsman; my shaman's leap into my new life?" I intently questioned the French girl, staring directly into her ethereal eyes. She stared back perplexed.
I stared up at the statue, at Gibson's strong face, and considered the odorous task blessed upon me by my relative and the faery. With a deep breath, an unsteady step, and fanatical grin I climbed the statue of the Gibson-William-Wallace and I spanked the freedom into the Gibbon with the cardboard broadsword.

"Freedom," I screamed, as the flash went off on the camera

"Freedom," I screamed again, as my Uncle and Mademoiselle Frenchie-Gray-Eyes cheered and danced.

"Freedom," I screamed with vigor, sword spanking stone ass, as a Stirling constable walked up and started shouting, "Oi Laddie! Whit ayre ye deein'?"

"Freedom!" I screamed, "Wallace is free!"

My Uncle grabbed my leg and shook me off the statue and gripped me in a tight bear hug, "I've got him, constable. I've got the wee young bastard! Ach! Ya dumb, young bastard. You're slapping the arse of a hero, son! "

"Mel Gibbons?" I sputtered as he began to drag me away.

"Mel Gibbons, I'b sorry, I'b sorrrry. Save me!"

In the distance I could hear the siren cackle of the French girl as she ran to her hostel. "That's what you get for messing with the Faery folk," was all that Uncle said to me as he hauled me to the drunk tanks with the constable.

I woke up in jail the next morning. Everything hurt and I was still very drunk. Next to me was another town drunk that'd soiled himself, and his blanket, while having half fallen onto the floor from his cot. I got up and called for water. It took awhile but finally I got some as I saw my Uncle striding in to collect me. He passed the constable a thicker-than-usual envelope as he walked up to me. Didn't even try to hide it.

He was carrying a pink flamingo and was wearing a Scottish tweed suit and a half kilt. He looked freshly shaven and alert but had a slight wobble in his step.

As we walked out of the constable's office, I noticed several pictures were posted on the window—pictures of me slapping the statue of William Wallace on his stone arse. Mel Gibson's scowl was piercing, malevolent, and dominating. As we walked out, my Uncle handed me several wallets. I opened them to see the Australians faces looking back at me before I dropped them and threw up in Craig's Alley.

"Ah, we're a wee bit sick are we? Time for a Scottish breakfast!"

As we walked, my Uncle breathing in deeply, shouted loudly, "Can you smell what Bob Ross is cooking? Is it rashers?

Bangers? Eggs? Toast!? Oh it's a beautiful smell old Bob is cooking up - A smell to paint the land of Scotland by. You see, here, sight isn't enough. We get bored using our eyes. Here everything is about the nose and the pull of the groin." He looked to me and grinned, "if Bob Ross were worth anything he'd paint a breakfast that'd feed the world over! Ya, hear that, boyo? Each brushstroke a different morsel of food on the canvas of breakfast!

All I could muster was a quiet and hollow, "... motherfucker..."

I bought a bus ticket to Edinburgh that afternoon, rented a hostel room for the remainder of my stay and hid. At the sound of a bottle I would shiver and hide myself in my duvet. Scotland had me afraid. I was wary of the faery folk with their whisky kisses and ocean eyes. I was lucky enough to get a copy of *Ivanhoe* from someone at the hostel and I hid and didn't come out until I went to the airport.

Later that week, my uncle sent me an e-mail with several news stories. They had a picture of me spanking William Wallace with the caption, "Tourist Spanks Scotland's Willy." It was fairly detailed and made it clear that pictures were on sale at local tourist shops. The next article described how the community council had decided to build a fence around the statue so nothing demeaning could happen to it again. Uncle Illia was cited as the council member behind the motion. I could hear his deep, phlegm filled laugh behind the picture.

"Why in the seven, blooming hells would you want to be a Scot? We got the grippe in our bones, the heather tangled in our arses, and the natural inclination to arch our eyebrows evilly towards the oxen heads of this world's ill-bred men."

I still don't get it. I don't. I mean I just told you what happened, and it did happen, but I still don't get it. I guess there's something I can't explain in words, how, although it scared me, spanking Mel Gibson's ass felt like I was liberating Scotland for everyone; that the land no longer had to live under the Gibbon King of Scotland.

I'm at a loss. What the fuck happened?

FALL FROM GRACE

Stich

Working construction on this highrise condo in midtown Manhattan certainly had its share of perks. Not only did I pocket some good change, with four and a half years of steady work at $48 an hour, but the daily reward of having built the second tallest building in New York City (and the country) made me proud to be an American. Only the New World Trade Center would look down upon us. For the son of a German immigrant, I'd done good, even though I only made it to the ninth grade.

The Alfred P. Grace Center at 1590 feet (106 floors) is only four stories shy of 'the trade center', and three stories taller than the Empire State Building. How Commissioner Grace had managed to push his 'pet monstrosity' through the local government is truly a testament to his persuasive charm, and of course, having deep pockets of 'family money' didn't hurt. The City Commissioner was running for Mayor next fall and completing this project was crucial in his election plans.

Tomorrow, the grand opening of the Center, would put Alfred in the limelight like never before. Dignitaries from around the country, including Vice President Pawlenty, were coming to pay homage to the 'house that Alfred built'. The building had garnered lots of support, since it had been touted and portrayed as a 'cultural center' for minorities, with one floor so designated. But a hundred floors of condos consumed the structure, with the penthouse floor entirely devoted to a gym containing the latest work-out equipment, and the whole 45th floor was a 24-hour food court.

The building was complete, with only one task remaining: to remove the canvas covering the statue at the very top, for the grand opening. A small group of us construction workers had gathered on the roof of the penthouse for this last job. Every day we had worked on this building our foreman would barbeque lunch for us. Today was no different, only the odor today was that of premium-cut steaks. Johnny, my friend and co-worker noticed.

"Can you smell what Bob Ross is cooking?" he said.

"It sure ain't hotdogs and hamburgers again." I said with my mom's Norwegian accent.

"We'll eat after you guys get that canvas off!" Bob shouted.

We all looked up at the canvas, covering the 75-foot tall statue.

"I'll do it", I said, sensing reluctance from my work buddies.

I grabbed the safety harness, put it on, and attached the lanyard. We had kept a hydraulic 'cherry picker' with a 100-foot reach, on the roof for this final job. Jumping in the bucket, I immediately clipped the lanyard to the bucket rail and gave the operator a thumb's up. While being lifted skyward, I gazed out over Manhattan, never tiring of this view, it was the usual... breathtaking skyline!

When I reached the top, dangling front and center of the statue, I motioned for the bucket operator to hold. About 3 feet in front of me was the canvas release. All I had to do was pull on it, and the canvas should fall to the roof of the penthouse. I pulled, and pulled, and pulled with all my might, but it wasn't releasing.

Being a proud German-Norwegian, with more brawn than brain, I braced both my feet against the statue, with my back on top of the bucket, and gave a Herculean tug on the release. Two things happened at once: The release opened, and a nesting pigeon burst into my face. The momentum I had from pulling on the release, coupled with the bird in my face, forced me to tumble backwards, over, and out of the bucket.

I heard a scream (which was my own) as I began to sail out over the side of the building. At that same moment I realized I had the lanyard attached to the rail, and it would soon "catch" and I'd be dangling. For a second, I felt embarrassed in front of my friends (for the scream) but as I watched the lanyard slack tighten, and then the bucket railing it was attached to suddenly break free, my embarrassment turned to horror. I was heading downward with no way of stopping.

For the next few moments, everything seemed as though it were moving in slow motion. My momentum from the 'big' tug carried me over the edge of the penthouse roof. I stared at my open-mouthed, soon-to-be ex-coworkers, as I slipped past the edge of the building and started plummeting towards the street. With a last glance upward, I saw the statue. It was a huge rendition of our benefactor, Commissioner Grace, complete with a stocky torso, hairless head, and a big cigar hanging out of his mouth (he always smoked a cigar).

It would take 4.6 seconds for my body to travel the nearly 1600 feet to the ground. A calm feeling of terror had come over me. Perhaps more like a bit of reluctant acceptance that I was soon to be a red blotch on the pavement. While flying past the penthouse, there, only 5 feet from me, in the huge window of the yet-to-be-opened work-out center was a naked woman. It was Mary, one of the housemaids I had flirted with. She had her hands on the window, with her bare breasts squeezed against the glass looking like a pair of 'eggs over easy'. Standing directly behind her was none other than Alfred P. Grace. He too, was totally naked, with cigar in mouth and apparently giving Mary some sausage to go with those eggs. Both their eyes began to bug-out as they glimpsed me passing by. I hope I wrecked his 'moment', that wife-cheating bastard.

When I passed the 60th floor, I had reached terminal velocity. At 120 miles per hour it would only be 2.2 more seconds before I made contact. With what, I wondered, as I looked straight down. A fast-growing orange rectangle began to take shape below me. I could see a blinking white light on top. Then I realized, "Oh my God, it's a school bus!" With no time to maneuver, I just prayed no kids were on board.

With barely a hundred feet to go, I closed my eyes, and braced for the inevitable shattering of my body. And then, I hit.

Smash! I became an "Instant Norwegian Pancake", with a bit of German spice splattered around!

FEVERS OF THE LIVING

Alexander Helmke

I decide to be celibate when she recalls the exact amount of an abortion in dollars, that she has a second savings account for such emergencies. How many emergencies? I say as the condom rag-dolls into the trashcan. About two, she says. Her name is Elise and this isn't going to last long. She lives with two pastors on their third floor. They're the cool kind, the kind that store a Bible on the top shelf, bourbon and gas station cigars on the counter. People that would lean over at your execution and say, you can come to heaven, sure, why not. Elise asks does this mean we're done and I say I don't know. We'll talk. She says okay and I leave.

At the bus stop I call my dad to tell him about my life decision. He's a senator at the statehouse downtown. All he says about his work is that there are still laws because there's still money. He looks like a composer locked up in a tower, hair askew. He is German and once spoke it fluently until my grandfather died, is clean-shaven and works in an office with carved woodwork.

Dad picks up the phone.

"Oh yeah, come on. Tell me what you want."

"It's Mike."

A silence.

"Senator Robert Ross, speaking?"

"Mike. Your son."

"Oh hey Michael, hey guy. I know who you are. A page is doing something for me on the other line. You caught me at a time," he says.

I hear clicking, the shuttering of windows.

"I want to talk to you. I'm going to be celibate," I say. "For a while."

"Oh, whose birthday? Do I know them?"

"I have decided not to have sex," I say.

A blond woman with a rolling bag walks past me, the wheels on the sidewalk slabs measuring her pace. There are jeans and parts moving under them. She's the right kind of lost. I guess I have to look away now.

"Oh like a monk? Or like your mother by the end?"

He laughs. They have been divorced for about a year. He's fully German and always said that she ruined his family line with her Tory eggs.

"I'm going to stop by," I say.

This guy waiting with me wearing a lanyard and a baseball cap with a white curtain covering his neck shouts about the scantily clad photograph selling clothes on the side of the bus, how fine she is, how dirty she is, how she leads him to dark places of his heart.

My grandfather, in his final days, would say Germany can't lose this war, they are a good people. We've come from a strong line. He thought the help button on the side of the hospital bed was an elevator. He flirted with the nurses, saying that he was heading home to this penthouse suite with a nice view, that they should join him. It has a nice view, like from here, he said as the nurse bent over to change some bag filled with him.

We learned about the printing press in school at the time and I thought of him helping Johannes with the first one. That's how old he seemed to me. He'd have a mouthful of sauerkraut spilling and spilling onto the minted pages like some Old Testament miracle. Old Johannes would get mad at grandpa's krauted pages, yell at him in fluent German. He would say, you stupid fuck, my device is going to change Germany. Germany will do no harm. We are a peaceful people now that we can read. My grandfather nods and says we will be the best in that high baby voice, like a rewinding tape.

A small protest group is holding signs and walking ovals around the capitol steps. A handcrafted sign in permanent marker says CAN YOU SMELL WHAT BOB ROSS IS COOKING? They chant something that rhymes hugs with drugs. My father authored the bill to make certain hallucinogens legal, the ones that don't melt your brain.

He says it's our duty as Americans to remember, to expand brain capacity to what we can't see. He does not know that people laugh at him outside of his office, through forwarded emails and the like. He thinks he is respected.

I walk up the steps and cover my face like the sun is bright, but it isn't.

My father is putting with a machine that spits the ball back. He has a mini piano that plays by itself. The volume control is broken, classical music blares.

"You are here early," my dad says. "The bus was on time? They're trying to ban buses, you know."

"To what?"

"Ban them. Morally, you know."

"No, no I don't know," I say.

"The Republicans believe that buses are 'harbingers of moral disease.' Think there are better ways of helping the poor. Like giving them guns."

He laughs and misses his putt. It bounces off the paper shredder. His office smells like high school girls on a field trip to a museum.

"I ride the bus," I say.

"Hell, of course you do. All sorts of people ride the bus. I'd ride it if I didn't have a car. You are a hippie. Just like I was."

"They still make those?" I say and point at the golfing machine.

Over on his desk he had an Atlas statue holding up one of those electrical balls that you plug in and see the bones in your hands in magenta and fuchsia hues. A science lab gave it to him as a gift, the one that wants to make illegal drugs legal.

"So what did you want to talk to me about?" Dad says.

"I forgot. Nothing."

"Oh, Mike-guy, there's this party tonight I want you to come to. News anchors will be there, pretty good looking. Firm asses and such. So I hear."

"Oh yeah. I'm celibate," I say.

"So you can't drink? You can't have a drink? Are you my son?" He tries to take my temperature with the back of his palm. I swat him away. He raises his hands and yells and his arms flail like he's challenging lightning.

"Fine," I say.

"Bring a friend or something," he says. "Oh that's right, you're not fucking."

He has the smile a dentist couldn't replicate, teeth gallows straight. I left and behind me he said something about touching base.

I tell Elise to meet me at a coffee shop close to the capitol. There are pictures on the walls, one is of this black guy on a stoop. It's called *Jazz* and costs two hundred dollars. It looks fuzzy so I take it off the wall and shake it to see if it develops.

A barista tells me I can't do that. She's cute but looks homeless, like she is looking for somewhere to be, bandana holding unwashed hair. I put the picture back in its place and nothing has changed about it. The local paper in a wire rack has a picture of the guy holding that sign about dad's bill. The headline says "Is Senator Ross Tripping?" I'm at a table thinking if I will ever be him, about ancient desert fathers and wet dreams while wearing a robe. Elise sees me and sits down.

"I have been looking for you for twenty minutes. I called you like eight times."

I don't check my phone.

"Okay," I say.

Elise is too thin but I can't say anything about that. I know she has weight issues. She dances. I don't know what healthy thin is. I tell her about the party at the manor. She looks at the newspaper on the table.

"That's your dad?" Elise says.

"Yeah."

I move the newspaper to a different table.

"Wow."

"Bad wow, or good wow?" I say.

"Just wow."

I break my stirring stick into a square and arrange it into a rhombus, one of the few shapes I remember from any math class.

"Did you come?" she says.

"Well, the party is tonight," I say.

"Last night, you and me."

An old woman is reading a novel with a beach cottage on the cover. She sets it down like a tent and looks at us.

"Um, yeah," I say. "Sure."

"Well you did, so congrats."

"Is the condom okay?" I say like asking how a vacation was.

"Nothing happened," she says.

"So why are we talking about this?"

"Because I miss you."

"It's been a day," I say.

"Not even, and that's what's so hot."

She doesn't look beautiful with the sun on her pale skin, the black hair in her face like a girl sitting and pouting on the side of a mall planter. The music overhead sounds tribal, like if natives could find outlets in the sand for distorted guitars.

I was going to meet Elise's family tonight, but now that isn't going to happen. She knows this and doesn't say anything. I've known her a month, why do I have to meet her family?

I tell her I can't do it.

"What? Oh my god. Do us? This?"

"See your family," I say.

The cute, homeless barista clutches and cleans the milk steamer by rubbing it with a damp cloth.

"All right. So, how's celibacy going? When can I see you again?"

"It's been one day," I say.

My mother said that he was never like this, your father. He was so reserved, he did what he was told. Then your grandfather's mind went and died. That man was like the Fourth Reich to him, she said.

I don't think she knew what that meant.

Your father got distant, stopped talking to me and then started thinking about drugs and liberation. He started thinking about the elderly, she said and laughed. She was arranging fake flowers in water, marbles bouncing at the bottom of the vase.

"He used the belt, you know, your grandfather."

I picked at the eggs she cooked. They were brown on the edges like old envelopes, the kind that taste like glue for days.

"Well, he is German," I said. "*Achtung* and all that."

"I'm glad I don't have his name anymore," she said, like I was in another room.

At the party Dad stands alone in a corner looking at a painting. The strokes are epileptic, no vanishing point. I tell him this and he turns around.

"It's all color and color and color," he says. "There is no subject. In anything."

"I think people are talking about you," I say. Half of his cocktail napkin is bunched. His nose hair could grow to be a mustache. He is wearing a suit with coattails.

"Oh, they always are. It's the parade I am in. Politics, here's to you." A small puddle of wine is staining the bottom of the glass. "Please take care of this. And for your sake, get yourself something."

I refill his glass. The table is filled with wine, dated labels like a chronology line in a history book. One is older than me and unopened.

A woman approaches me. She's wearing a three-finger ring, brass knuckles for women.

"What date is your destiny?" she says.

"The white one, 2004, I guess." I say.

"I'd say that's a good choice, but I don't have any idea what the hell any of it means."

"Yeah," I say.

"Fay," she says and sticks out her hand.

"Mike," I say. We shake hands like we're holding them.

She's wearing a short blue dress that contorts like a question. We stand there.

"Before you ask me what I do," she says, "I'm an anchor. You know. For the news."

I've seen her forget her cues and talk about murder. She's wearing lip-gloss, which makes her mouth look like the inside of a seashell, unreachable. Don't think about what her mouth does. She asks me what I do, what I like.

"I'm a student, or was. Graduated."

I dropped out.

"Oh, what?"

"Media studies. Communication."

History then Drama then Art and then Leave.

"Sounds familiar."

I don't know why she's talking to me. I realize I am holding and not drinking two cups of wine.

"There you are, wine boy," he says. I can't tell if there's another bar in the house.

"Oh Robert," Fay the Anchor says. "How do you know this young man?"

"He's my sperm," he says. "From a long time ago."

Dad laughs and stares at the wine selection.

She looks at me. She takes a sip.

"Don't try anything," he says. "He's celibate."

Dad walks off to join a group talking about him. Their voices change. Fay refills her glass again.

"I wish your father would be celibate."

"Pardon?" I say.

"He loves the page program," she says and walks away.

Dad wasn't there the night his father died. I was little. I did not know what it all meant. My grandfather told me from his hospital bed that our last name was changed on the boat here, an umlaut to an *o*, something easier to say. Roose sounds like noose, he said and laughed, looked off into the distance. He always talked about Germany like nothing happened, that there was a hole in the timeline, history books have it all wrong, look what has come from there, he said and hit his heart with his fist like an actor playing a Roman. Look, he said and patted where his heart was trying.

As I walk to the porch people talk about Dad's bill. How it's stupid, unfounded, unpassable. They recite newspapers and signs and say for once the protesters are right. They talk about his corner office and the toys he receives from future legal drug labs. They laugh. They don't know who I am. Someone says I can't understand why he has a job, has he ever done any drug or does he know what they do?

The porch is made of cobblestone and no weeds poke through.

Fay is smoking a cigarette.

"I'm drinking, what can I say," she says. "I have a pretty voice during the week. We are not in the week."

"Has my father ever tried anything?" I say.

"I can give you names. I'm good with names."

"I mean drugs, I guess."

"Oh god, I don't know. He's crazy and fun, just the thing to have around."

I want there to be cherubs peeing in a pool but there's

no fountain, only dark green expanding until the iron blur of
fence. Only croquet stakes litter the lawn.

"Sorry what I said about the pages earlier. I didn't mean
just anyone. He likes girls, don't worry. I mean, sorry. I'm not
like this. I like everyone. I love people." She holds the stem of
her glass like a pencil.

I think about his armchair talks with my mother. He
would scream in German when I was up in my room. I thought
there was an emergency or I was in trouble. He threw things,
too. Buckets and hoses and stools, usually nothing breakable.
She said you stupid fucking Hun once while he stormed
out, slamming the door, car engine starting then distant like
cartoon sounds. It made me laugh at the time, the sound of
what the words didn't mean. Now I don't know what to think.

"So," Fay says. "Why are you celibate? When did that
happen?"

"Today."

"Today?"

"Yeah."

"Why?" She says and stands closer to me.

"I wanted something different," I say.

"So you want a challenge?" she says.

I'm sober-drunk teetering on pronouncing every
syllable. She has a great body. Don't think about bodies.

My father leans out the double white doors and
whispers to me.

"Michael, they are laughing at me," he says. "The
bill will pass. I know it will. We can remember, we must
remember."

I tell Fay I'm sorry for that, sorry about him.

She stubs the cigarette on the marble railing and walks
inside. I follow later.

Inside my father grabs my shoulder.

"I think they are talking about me. I know they are. My hearing isn't what it once was, I think."

"Then why are you here, why am I here?" I say.

"To be noticed. To save memories. To make a difference."

"I'm leaving," I say.

"But you just arrived, it's just starting."

Servants or something are cleaning up empty things. Dishes of nuts and plates of seafood clatter in carried stacks. People place both arms through their coat sleeves.

"They are still talking about me, I can hear them," he says.

I walk him out to his car and hope he remembers how to drive. I pat the top of the car twice and don't know why.

The bus doesn't run this late so Elise picks me up. She says sorry about the coffee shop, about freaking out. I threw up a few times after we talked, that's all. I'm just nervous you'll leave.

Her car smells like melted crayons, vacuum tracks crisscross the floor mats.

"But yeah, anyway. I have this married friend, she pin pricked condoms so her husband wouldn't know."

"That's strange," I say.

"Sex should be fun. Not devious, you know?"

I think about my grandfather in his hospital bed, pressing and pressing the assist button he thought could take him anywhere. I know he was losing his mind. I want to be there again to tell him what I've seen, that I can make Germany proud again. That I am strong, but I'm not. I'll tell him I'll never be like his son and I saved him from something bad, or will, whatever. I'll do all of it in fluent German.

All I want is to shake with fevers of the living.

Pussybreath Johnson

Jamie Quinn Jefferson

And I had just made up my mind that very morning.
This type of coincidence happens to me all too often for it to
be any type of real coincidence, I do realize that. It might be the
whiskey running through my Irish blood, the delirium tremors
that I pass off as a sign from God. I suppose it *could* even be
God, that bastard. I've sworn him off whilst cussing him out
my entire life and he might just have been slappin' me in my
Irish nut sack the whole time, getting a real kick out of my
general bewilderment. I understand the pattern of events that
take place when I will such an occurrence into being. The logic
appears written in bold Times New Roman across my forehead,
only noticed in the mirror immediately *after* said coincidence
occurs.

Nonetheless, I really, really, actually decided one
hundred percent that very morning that I would live out the
rest of my life without ever again breaking into a lingerie shop
to relieve my bowels on top of the service desk. I'm sure you've
heard of me, The Panty Shop Shitter. It started off as a prank in
college, of course. Since then I've shat in more undergarment
establishments than I care to recall. The fact that I've never
been caught is miraculous enough, not to mention the strange
amount of undeserved respect I've received from friends and
acquaintances, male and female alike. These things had kept

me in the game thus far, that is, until that one morning when superstition got the best of me.

I've always been a superstitious bloke. Once when I was quite young I witnessed a whistling girl tending to a crowning hen. When a black cat walked out of the barn towards the girl, I threw up and passed out. Another time, a young woman I had been dating offered me a lock of her hair as a token of her committed love for me. I actually rather liked this one, but still couldn't help breaking up with her immediately, throwing up a bit as I did. And then there were the vivid dreams. The dreams that appear more real than anything I experience while awake. In this one particular dream, Jesus walked up to me while I was at a mall's food court.

Jesus said, "Hey dude. You better stop shitting in panty shops. I'm serious. Something bad is going to happen. Fair warning. Alright, later dude."

I woke up that morning and I felt like a new man. I was no longer The Panty Shop Shitter. It was going to be easy to avoid any situation that might be conducive to shitting in a panty shop, because, well, Jesus himself had given me fair warning. And if I had caught anything my mother had ever told me between drunken burps and cackles, it was to listen to Jesus when he appeared at a mall food court in one of your vivid dreams. Yes sir, I was done with that childish business.

It had not been eight hours since I had convinced myself that I need not joke with such tomfoolery any longer. Not even eight hours before he appeared from behind a dumpster in the alleyway of *Brut de Decoffrage*. One look and I knew he was trouble. I stopped to light a fag when the sound of his leather Prada's against the asphalt startled me. The overwhelming warmth of déjà vu washed over my chest and face as he smiled and walked toward me. I had seen this smile before. I see this smile almost every day of my life. He coughed once before addressing me.

"Didn't mean to startle you, bud."

His hair was messed up. It had no doubt been sprayed to perfection earlier, but he'd run his hand through, making it stand about this way and that. He was smaller than me, broad shoulders atop a medium frame, dangerous brown eyes sunken into a soft, dark face. He was still smiling as he reached his hand towards mine.

"Samuel Anderson." His hand was cold and firm. He maintained a polite handshake for just the right amount of time. I felt comfortable in his grasp.

"Pussybreath. Pussybreath Johnson," I said.

It just came out of me like I had absolutely no control over my tongue or my mouth or any aspect of this encounter at all. Samuel giggled. I could tell he was thoroughly entertained by my introduction. He wasn't laughing uncomfortably or smiling out of estranged politeness, he was giggling like I giggle when laughter feels so good that my stomach decides to take the pleasures of amusement to another level.

"Well it's a pleasure to meet you, Mr. Johnson. Forgive me, but I must ask about the origin of such a terrific forename."

"God-given, believe it or not." I was still speaking on auto-pilot. I had left the confines of my body and now stood just left of my smart mouth, watching this conversation unfold as if it were on a silver screen.

"I was destined to be woman's one true pleasure."

"That's quite a bit of pressure," Samuel said as the smile dropped from his face. He began feeling the breast pockets of his suit jacket as he continued, "Destinies are tricky buggers, aren't they? Improbable to fulfill, impossible to outlive." Samuel found a small joint in his coat pocket and brought it up to his lips.

"Punching out for the day," he said with a gentle smirk. "No time cards in my line of work. I've found having a smoke is a real nice bookend to another half-ass day on the job."

I saw myself light my own fag before making the conscious decision to slip back into my body.

"What line of work are you in, Samuel?" I asked.

"Politics."

"Ha! And who isn't?" I laughed.

"Ha," Samuel didn't really laugh. He lit his joint, inhaled quickly and peaked around the corner of the restaurant. He drew in a practiced French inhale and replied,

"I guess you could say I was destined to be the people's one true miser."

"Ah! A republican. My kind of man," I said.

"So I can count on your vote come November then?" Samuel uttered sarcastically.

"What are you running for?" I asked.

"Exercise," he replied bluntly.

I giggled.

"Seriously," he said. Samuel's tone had changed. He was no longer the smart ass that began this conversation. His face suddenly looked much older.

"What are you, Pussybreath, Irish?" Samuel asked.

"How did you know?" I quietly muttered, lungs full of smoke.

"Your eyes, your eyebrows."

I exhaled deeply.

"That, and the fact that you reek of Irish whiskey!"

At that we both hooted and slapped our knees in amusement.

"They should call you Boozeybreath." Samuel said with a smirk.

"Good one," I laughed.

"You know, the real charm of my name, of course, is in the irony. I'm actually super gay."

Samuel nearly fell over at that one. When he had finally collected himself, he tossed his joint to the curb. He turned to read me square in the eye.

"I'm a confused man, Pussybreath. I lead quite the lifestyle, you know? But to no avail."

"I don't follow, Samuel."

"I'm a ringer. Of sorts. I don't know. I don't know what I am."

"I have no idea what you're talking about man," I laughed.

"I've been hired to take a fall before the Primaries in order to make that asshole Austin look better."

"You'll have to excuse me, Samuel, but I don't follow politics in the least. Take a fall? Like in a boxing match?"

"Yeah like in a fucking boxing match," Samuel replied quickly and with anger in his voice. He caught himself and perked up a bit. Taking a deep breath he explained,

"I'm a fraud, Pussybreath. I go around town meeting all sorts of important people and making positive impressions at all the right times. I've got a clean history so I'm exactly the type of schmuck that they approach for these sorts of things. They find some young wannabe politician that doesn't have enough money to run for office and they tell me that I'll get all the experience of the political game and even come out of it a richer man than I when I entered. And then they tell you some guy named Big Frankie is gonna kill your girlfriend if you don't take a fall in the sixth round."

Now I was genuinely interested.

"And how do you 'take a fall,' exactly?" I asked.

"Oh, you know, you get busted with a bunch of drugs, or you get caught banging your secretary or you, uh, you know, you break into some panty shop and get caught on tape dropping trow on the fucking cash register. You alright Pussybreath?"

I had swallowed some spit down the wrong pipe and was caught in a fit of coughing.

"Excuse me. I though you said something about breaking into a panty shop." I replied.

"Yeah, man! Surely you've heard of the Panty Shop Shitter!" Samuel now had a huge grin on his face. "What a character, you know. Something real charming about that guy you can't really put your finger on. You heard about that guy a couple years ago, right?"

"Yeah I heard about him." I replied, trying to maintain some level of normal facial expression.

"Yeah that's the way I would want to go. If I gotta take a fall then I want it to be doing something awesome."

The wind picked up. We were standing in a dead-end alley way and yet the wind swept cold beneath our feet. I looked up towards the sky for a moment, by the time I looked back Samuel was walking toward the middle of the street, his eyes directed towards a series of small shops a block away. I knew what was going to happen. I guess I kind of knew what was going to happen when my eyes locked with Samuel's five minutes earlier. I felt that familiar warmth of déjà vu before he had even uttered a word in my direction.

"Fuck. Man, Pussybreath! I feel alive right now. I feel more alive than I've felt in months!"

"Hey, why don't you settle down there, Mr. Anderson. That weed might have gotten to you a bit," I chuckled. "I think you're getting a little ahead of yourself there. What round is it, anyways? Think about your girlfriend."

"I ain't got no girlfriend!" Samuel spun around with his hands out and his face beaming. "I gave those suckers a picture of one my old girlfriends that killed herself years ago!" By this time Samuel was doing some sort of stretch, bouncing on the balls of his feet as if in preparation for some intense physical activity.

"I'm the only one going down in this mess, and if I'm going down, by God I'm going down taking a shit in the middle of a motherfucking panty shop!"

"Jesus Christ," I mumbled. I couldn't help but smile.

"So, what'll it be Pussybreath? Is you is or is you ain't my constituency?"

Samuel had already found a large garbage can and broken the picture window of the *Sexy Sexy* lingerie boutique by the time I had made my way down the block.

He screamed, "Motherfuckers!" as the glass shattered. The alarm went off, blaring louder than any I had ever encountered. Samuel looked back to see if I was behind him. I was shirtless, smiling from ear to ear.

"Hot damn!" he shouted as he jumped through the broken window. Samuel frolicked around the shop picking teddies off the racks and throwing them every which way. I, on the other hand, was already down to business. I had ripped my shirt and wrapped it around my head so that it formed my signature hood/veil. This image that with which the Panty Shop Shitter had become synonymous. I carefully climbed behind the register and on to a large folding counter.

"Alright, stop screwing around Samuel. You're going to want to start concentrating on moving your bowels. It's harder to shit under pressure than you might think."

Samuel turned and his face lit up as he pointed at me, "Hey! The Panty Shop Shitter! Nice, man!"
Samuel climbed up beside me and dropped his pants around his ankles. He squatted slowly and assumed the position. The alarm stopped. It became incredibly quiet for a moment as we

both focused on our bowels. Another moment passed. Samuel was breathing heavily. I could tell that I was going to be able to make good any moment now. Police sirens became audible in the distance.

Samuel let out a loud gasp before whispering, "Can you smell what Bob Ross is cooking?"

"What?" I gasped in amusement as my own bowel movement began the slow but steady departure from my asshole. The sirens were getting louder.

"Oh he's cooking it alright! Yep! And, here, we, go. BOOM!" Samuel continued to add vocal sound effects as he shit all over the folding counter. The volume of the sirens told me that the police were obviously just around the corner.

"What up bitches!" He exclaimed as he reached his hand in the air, gesturing for a high five. I slapped his hand before reaching for a pair of panties to wipe my ass with.

"Alright, let's get the fuck out of here."

"PUT YOUR HANDS IN THE AIR YOU SICK FUCKS!"

There were several police officers standing in front of the broken window, guns drawn. Samuel put his hands up, pants still around his ankles. He was giggling like a man who had completely lost his mind. I sighed, pulled my pants up and put my hands in the air. I knew we were going to get caught that night. Jesus told me so. Our Lord and Savoir went out of his way to give me fair warning, and I passed excrement on a lingerie shop service desk in spite of that. I should have listened to my mother. I should have listened to Jesus.

Story Directives

1. *Personal/Character jokes about heredity or genetic makeup*
2. *A corrupt politician*
3. *The line, "Can you smell what Bob Ross is cooking?"*